The Return of Jimmy Watson

Robber 1978

By
Frank Nash

Copyright © 2023 by Frank Nash

All rights reserved.

For Bernadette

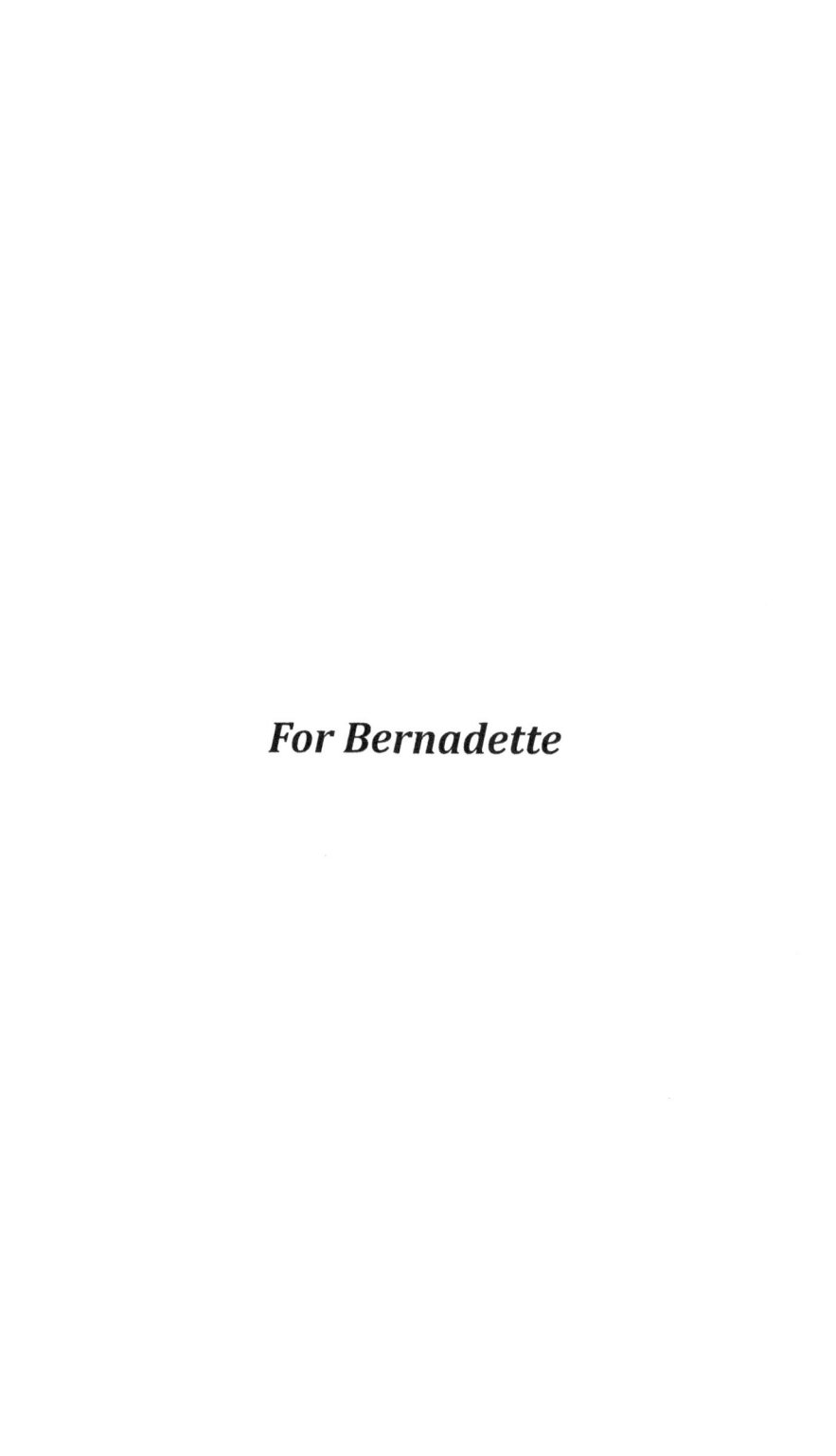

Contents

CHAPTER ONE	**1**
What Did I Do Last Night?	1
CHAPTER TWO	**17**
Dreadlock Holiday	17
CHAPTER THREE	**34**
Nutted by Reality	34
CHAPTER FOUR	**49**
Airport	49
CHAPTER FIVE	**58**
Mystery Dance	58
CHAPTER SIX	**70**
Grey Cortina	70
CHAPTER SEVEN	**90**
Down at the Doctor's	90
CHAPTER EIGHT	**101**
Message in a Bottle	101
CHAPTER NINE	**110**
With a Little Luck	110
CHAPTER TEN	**124**
Burn Baby Burn	124
CHAPTER ELEVEN	**134**
Holiday in The Sun	134
CHAPTER TWELVE	**146**
Two Out of Three Ain't Bad	146

CHAPTER ONE

What Did I Do Last Night?

The radio alarm clicked on.

"Good morning, it's seven o'clock and this is the BBC news."

Jimmy Watson, face down on the bed, opened his eyes and all he could see was blood. He could see it on the pillows and feel it on his face. He panicked and sat bolt upright. There was a thud as a red wine bottle rolled off the bed and nestled into the skirting board. He sighed with relief, realising he'd fallen asleep and an open Merlot had gone everywhere. The night before he'd been out but couldn't even remember where he'd been or who he'd been with.

The radio continued, "Morning, it's the breakfast show with your hairy cornflake, Dave Lee Travis. Yes, it's Monday, March the 27th and here's 'Peaches' by "The Stranglers."

"Fuckin' hairy cornflake," mumbled Jimmy.

"Deh, Deh Dun," came the opening bars of the song.

He reached over and pushed the radio off. He slumped back onto the bed and from somewhere he could hear a loud ticking.

It's that bloody carriage clock Julia's mother bought us, laughing at me!

He'd spent nine years in jail dreaming of a reconciliation with Julia, his ex, but after a euphoric reunion in the first passionate weeks, things started to change. They were no longer youngsters, both now nudging forty; they were wiser, choosier and they quickly noticed the flaws in each other. The carefree naïve girl he'd known in London was now a high-achieving businesswoman in Geneva, and he was an out of work ex-con. Dinner parties were awkward when the inevitable question came up: "*And what exactly do you do for a living?*" It was quite a conversation stopper.

Often, the subject of how he'd deceived her during their four years together would arise over dinner or in bed or just anywhere in private. It was the permanent elephant in the room that overshadowed their relationship more and more. The lovemaking went from nearly every day to maybe once a week. She'd tell him she was either too tired or just not in the mood. For Jimmy's part, although the rejection bothered him at first, even he'd got to a stage of apathy, realising their future wasn't together.

He'd always assumed that if he hadn't gone to prison, they would have been married with kids and it would have been happy families.

Christmas was a disaster. Their final argument was Jimmy accusing her of being embarrassed by him when they met her friends. He still felt out of step and out of time with everybody, but especially Julia. After six months in Switzerland, eating and drinking for England, he had no money left. He'd even got his dad to sell his beloved E-Type to help pay his way, but he knew he'd overstayed his welcome. The morning of his flight back to London, Julia had left early, to spare them both an awkward farewell. She'd left the sort of note you'd leave for a work colleague. He still loved her, but he wasn't "in love" with her, and he guessed she felt the same way about him. Their moment had passed.

So, this was it, back in England after almost a year since his release from ten years in a French prison.

In the past two weeks, he'd spent too much time on the booze feeling sorry for himself, pretending he was fine, but he wasn't. Last year, he liked seeing the grey skies, even the rain, but this time felt different.

England was in a much worse state twelve months on, with more strikes, rising unemployment and the ugly head of The National Front had reared. They were gaining support, especially in boroughs like Hackney and Barking in inner London. The Anti-Nazi League and Rock Against Racism were rallying against it. At the forefront were bands like The Clash and The Tom Robinson Band. At the same time, it was suspected that amongst the police, the NF had many sympathisers. Could this really be the country that fought the Nazis only thirty years before? What had happened to us?

Jimmy took off his wine-soaked clothes and shuffled naked into his bathroom, turning the bath taps on, yawning and scratching as he went to the kitchen to put the kettle on. He sat wearing nothing and staring into nothingness. A year ago, the thought of being with Julia again had kept him going. Then there'd been hope, now the only hope was no hope. Was it depression or self-pity? Whatever it was, he knew things had to change, especially as he had now run out of money. Apart from his flat, he had nothing left to sell. Jimmy slid into the bathtub with a mug of tea in his hand.

Half an hour later, he awoke with a startle. Someone was pressing the door buzzer and calling through the letter box. He got out of the bath and threw a dressing gown on and squelched his way to the front door.

"Morning Jimmy!"

"Oh, it's you!"

"Who did you expect, Jane Fonda?"

It was a smiling Handbag Bob. He followed Jimmy into the flat.

"Listen, thought I'd check on you as you were totally shit-faced last night."

"Where was I?"

"You really don't remember?"

"Nope."

"Jimmy mate, you've got to get your act together. You're a pisshead, this ain't you. Get someone in to clean this place up and while you're at it, clean yourself up as well. You look like you've just climbed off a fuckin' park bench."

Jimmy shrugged. Bob explained, "Your old man is worried sick about you!"

"He can talk when it comes to drinking!" He retorted.

"You two used to be thick as thieves Jimmy, what happened?"

"What fuckin' happened? Ten fuckin' years in prison happened! The joke is, if we got nicked now for that same robbery, we'd maybe get five years and out in three. Ten fuckin' years!"

"Well, that's all water under the bridge son. Listen, I know you're upset, what with things not working out with Julia, but you're acting like some soppy bird who's been ditched by her fella."

Handbag looked at his watch.

"Anyway Jim, sorry I gotta go, just wanted to see that you were all right."

"Where was I anyway?"

"You were with me and Ray at the Queen's in the high street. We dragged you home around midnight. Call me if you need me. You can even cry on my shoulder."

"Fuck off," Jimmy said with a chuckle. "Anyway, you still working in that call centre?"

Handbag grinned and looked around as if he was checking that he wasn't being overheard.

"Jimmy, I'm with a little crew and we've done a couple of Securicor vans and it's been a nice earner."

Jimmy frowned, "What – armed?"

"Well yeah, but only for show!"

"I've heard that one before. Aren't you worried about getting nicked?"

"Jimmy, it ain't like the 'sixties. Back then there were always a few bent cops, it's a different level now. You see, the City of London Police are not answerable to anyone. In that Square Mile are all the banks, all the financial institutions and newspapers, moving millions of pounds per week in vans. I'm telling you now, stick to working that area, and you can just about buy your way out of anything. There's geezers out there on bail for robbery set free to do even more robberies. It's down to the police to object to bail and they don't. The biggest gang in London are the cops, they're getting a fortune, it's a joke! They are a firm within a firm."

"Bob, you gotta be careful."

"Jimmy, I'm forty-two years old, all I've ever done is nick, it's all I know."

"But fuckin' armed robbery Handbag, you gotta get out of that!"

"We'll see... anyway, see you later Jim."

Bob left and, in his kitchen, Jimmy sat down and blew hard through his cheeks, alone in his thoughts. *Bob's into armed robbery. What the fuck is going on?*

He stared out of the window. The phone rang and he sat for a bit wondering who'd be calling him. He hesitantly picked up the receiver.

"Hello," he said in a croaky voice.

"Sounds like you've just woken up?"

"No, I've been up a while!"

Jimmy recognised the voice from long ago; it was Lesley Ward of Lloyd's Insurance.

There weren't many women like Ward at Lloyd's, in fact there weren't many women at Lloyd's. She was head of Fraud Investigations and had led quite an interesting life. After being de-mobbed from the WAF in 1946, she'd joined the company, and over the years had grown a labyrinth of contacts, in and out of the criminal world. She'd never married, her job was her life. Jimmy had known her since 1965, when she'd had a bit of a romance with a friend of his.

"James," (she always called him that), "I've been calling you for a couple of days, can you talk?"

"Yes, I learnt at a very young age."

"Still a joker. How are you?"

"I'm fine."

"Can you meet me at twelve today? I've got something that might interest you."

Jimmy leant against a door frame, working out the timings. "Er yes, sure, of course."

"Good, I'll book us a table at The Ritz. The maître de knows me."

"Is that a caff somewhere?"

"Very funny, it's The Ritz, as in Piccadilly. And Jimmy, don't forget, it's a shirt and tie job."

"Ok, I'll be there."

Jimmy put the phone down and thought for a moment. Well, as there wasn't actually a queue at his door offering opportunities, maybe a meeting might lead to something.

After countless cups of tea and half a dozen cigarettes, he put on a suit he'd bought whilst living with Julia. He'd kitted himself out from several stores in Geneva to impress her, but that obviously hadn't worked. The suit was brown with wide lapels and flared trousers. Under the jacket, he wore an orange shirt with a big collar and a wide beige tie. He put on a pair of burgundy slip-ons. He looked in the mirror. *Christ, I look rough*, he thought. Red eyes, dry skin and greying hair. *Time to cut down on the booze.* His hair needed a cut. He thought about Lesley; she'd been quite a looker back in the day, so he wondered how she looked now as it must have been twelve years since he'd last seen her.

As Jimmy made his way on foot across Primrose Hill, it was blowing a gale. The March weather had been exceptionally cold. A few brave tourists had made their way to the viewpoint, with one looking through a telescope, while the other looked at the chart that pointed out the sights across the skyline. The Post Office Tower glinted in the cold sunshine.

The Ritz Hotel dominates London's Piccadilly and is situated by Green Park Station and is every tourist's idea of "London luxury". By the time Jimmy got there, his face was reddened by the wind. An elderly doorman in a top hat addressed Jimmy.

"Can I help you Sir?"

"Yes, I'm having lunch with an old friend."

"No problem, just walk through to the young lady by the dining room."

Jimmy went through the large revolving doors and made his way to the Reception area that was busy with mainly American and Chinese tourists, cameras slung around their necks. The last time he had been here was in 1966, when, dressed in a dinner suit, he was about to relieve an Austrian couple of their valuables; how times had changed.

He reached the desk and a slim, elegant woman looked up.

"Morning Sir, are you dining with us today?"

"Yes, I'm meeting Miss Lesley Ward."

"Ah yes, please follow me Sir."

The dining room was busy with elderly couples dressed to the nines, most of whom were probably there, courtesy of a gift token that a family member would have bought them. She led him to where Ward was sitting. A glass of white wine, which she had already started, was on the table. She looked up.

"James." She politely stood up and put her hand out.

"Nice to see you. I understand you've been away from London for a long time."

"Lesley, you know full well where I've been for most of the past ten years!"

She gave a mischievous smile. "Yes, I did hear something. Turns out you weren't a mere jeweller when George and I used to see you with your girlfriend – Julia wasn't it?"

"Yes, that's right."

"Tell me, was it amusing knowing what I did for a living?" she asked.

"To be honest, I was shit-scared when I found out what you did, but I did like spending time with you. As I recall Lesley, Georgie got elbowed for some smooth Greek bloke at a party."

"Ah, you could be right," she said matter-of-factly.

A waiter pulled a chair back for Jimmy and laid a napkin across his lap. He handed him a menu and as he did so, asked,

"Aperitif, Sir?"

"A small beer please."

The waiter looked at him as if he'd just trodden on something unpleasant.

"We have one, I believe."

As he walked away, Jimmy said, "Anyone would think I'd asked for a rare Château."

Ward raised her glass.

"Cheers, good to see you. Hope you don't mind, but I've already ordered for both of us. I've got a meeting at 1.30."

"No that's fine, I like surprises." He was lying. *Bloody cheek,* he thought.

Ward had aged well, still attractive, now maybe sixty, but could easily pass for late forties. She was a lot thinner than he remembered. Elegant and well preserved, she was wearing a dark blue trouser suit with a white poplin blouse, she wore no jewellery. As far as he could see, she still had a nice figure; her hair was short and dyed blonde. The not-so-friendly waiter returned and poured the beer as if it was some precious vintage as opposed to a 75p lager.

Jimmy leant forward with both elbows on the table.

"Well Lesley, why did you want to see me?"

"Direct as always! I like that. We have a client, Peter Engels, who died in his Barbados restaurant two weeks ago. He also had a restaurant in London called The Fisheye and one in Rome, the name of which escapes me. He was quite flamboyant, married to a pretty formidable woman by all accounts. Sadly, our Mr Engels set light to himself and burnt to death in the restaurant kitchen, all pretty horrific. The thing is, only six months ago, he increased his life insurance cover to just over a million pounds. Now, he may have been just one very unlucky soul, but before we hand over that sort of money, we have to do some investigations of our own."

"Surely, you're not thinking he committed suicide – there's definitely easier ways to do it!"

"I agree, but we have to cross the T's and dot the I's, especially when the premium's been increased by so much, so recently. I'd like you to look at his death for me. Should be a piece of cake. Get out to Bridgetown, show your face, sign it off and come home."

"Lesley, if this was a robbery, I'd understand, but why are you asking me to look at an accident?"

"I'll be honest, Your name came up in an old address book of mine, going back to the old days. I remembered you'd served in the military police in Kenya in the early sixties, and I have to admit I was a little curious as to where you'd got to. I asked around and heard about your release last year. With your background Jimmy, where you've worked on both sides of the law, you would be perfect for us. When you left the service, maybe you should have become a nice constable rather than a robber!"

"A bit late for that I'd say, wouldn't you?"

"Life's all about turning left or right. We might make a detective out of you yet, Jimmy. Cheers," she raised her glass. She leant forward.

"Look, the Barbadian police say there's nothing suspicious, a tragic accident. It'll be an easy two day's work, you'd be a sort of poacher-cum-game keeper. It's something simple to cut your teeth on. Plus, I've got this."

Ward pushed a plastered leg out from under the table and tapped it with a dessert spoon.

"Broke my ankle skiing a few weeks back in Tiens. Jimmy, it's an easy two-day jaunt for five hundred pounds plus expenses, and if it goes well, we could look at doing more work together. Look upon it as a sort of audition and at the same time, you will also be doing me a great favour."

Jimmy smiled again; he couldn't deny Barbados was very appealing, and he could do with the distraction anyway to get him out of London and all the drinking, plus the money was much needed.

"Ok, when do you want me to go?"

"You've got a passport?"

"Of course!"

"Tomorrow?"

He thought for a moment.

"I can do that."

"Excellent. I will get Amanda, my PA, to ring you later to make arrangements."

The food arrived and the waiter, with great drama, removed the lid from a silver salver, which revealed a ridiculously small dinner. Jimmy looked at Ward.

"I think I'm gonna need a bag of crisps on the way home!"

CHAPTER TWO

Dreadlock Holiday

A black cab picked up Jimmy at 9.30 the following morning. The driver was a bearded Asian man who, on the journey, told Jimmy his life story, how he'd found God and that he had seven kids and hoped to go home to Kashmir within five years to keep horses. Funny who you can meet on a cab ride! As Jimmy got out at Heathrow, he turned to the cabbie and said, "I hope you get your dream!"

"Thank you, my friend," he shouted through the car window and then pulled away.

The airport was thankfully quiet, but it had changed dramatically since Jimmy was last here in the 'sixties. It was bigger with more and more shops.

Once aboard the plane, Jimmy found himself in what is every traveller's nightmare. The good news on one side was he had a very attractive blonde of around thirty, the bad news was on the other side, he had a crying baby in the arms of a very big woman with another crying baby in the row in front of him. They either cried together, or took turns. He smiled at the girl next to him, who acknowledged him with a grin. She put her headphones on.

The drinks trolley came along after around an hour. He ordered a Scotch and water, and the stewardess handed him a sachet which amongst the baby screams he thought she had said was ice. *"So clever, ice in a bag,"* he said smiling to the blonde next to him.

To his horror, he poured salted peanuts into his drink. He tried to conceal them with his hand and acted as though pouring nuts into a drink was the most natural thing to do. *Jesus, she must think I'm some sort of nut*, he thought to himself. Jimmy tried to shut out the baby's cries, whilst attempting to balance his drink and eating school dinner standard food. If only he'd pushed Lesley for first class! After several more torturous baby-filled hours, the *Fasten Seat Belts* sign came up and the captain welcomed the passengers to Barbados.

"Bad news everyone. There's been a front of bad weather that's hit the island and the temperature is only fifteen degrees."

The whole plane groaned in disappointment. Then there was a chuckle over the intercom.

"And as you've probably guessed, it's April Fools' day today!" A universal sigh of relief went around the cabin.

As Jimmy stood on the steps of the plane, the blast of hot air almost felt like a hair dryer being switched on. The weather was fabulous. As he came through the departure gate, various porters in search of tips, asked if they could carry his bag, but he politely turned them down. Jimmy stood under the circular canopy of the airport that reminded him of old bus stations in the north of England.

Before leaving London, Jimmy had contacted Andy McKay, which was a very unusual name for a six-foot two-inch Barbadian. The other mystery was the fact he spoke with a very plummy accent and sounded more like a BBC announcer, rather than a man schooled in the West Indies. Jimmy had been good friends with him in his military police days in Nairobi. They'd met in the early sixties when racial prejudice was the norm, but Andy had weathered the insults and had proved the doubters wrong, (some in his own family). He stayed in the army for eleven years and rose to the rank of sergeant. After that, he'd lived in Camden for a couple of years and had then returned to Barbados in 1972, where he'd become a taxi driver, mainly picking up tourists from the airport or taking them on tours.

As Jimmy came out of the airport, standing next to a black 1967 Austin Cambridge was Andy.

"Blimey! My dad used to have one of these. Still remember the number plate, NMP 345."

"Well, the older clients like it, reminds them of back in the day when we had to bow and scrape!"

Andy threw his hand into Jimmy's.

"Great to see you man."

"Sorry I'm late Andy."

"Listen, in Barbados, you're never late!"

They both laughed.

"Lloyd's have booked me into the Colony Club."

"Very nice," smiled Andy.

The drive was around forty-five minutes on recently tarmaced roads, passing new-builds, old colourful houses and some bungalows that looked like they could fall down at any moment.

The two chatted comfortably, as the car pulled onto the M1 heading towards Holetown.

"Have you heard of a guy called Peter Engels, who owned a restaurant called The Plantation?" Jimmy asked.

"Restaurant is very popular, we just passed it back there. Let me ask around." Replied Andy.

The Colony Club is situated in the Parish of St James on the West Coast of the Island. Here the Caribbean Sea is much calmer than the Atlantic on the south of the island. Originally it was set up as a club for mainly white employees of the British Army and the Government back in the 1940s. The area has been long favoured by ex-pats and tourists. The entrance to the club is white-walled and opposite are some run-down shacks – you couldn't get more of a contrast in fortunes if you tried. Just past the shacks is the road to West Moreland where the well-to-do live or have holiday homes.

The car pulled along the palm tree lined drive, turning left into a small carriage driveway in front of the hotel. Andy got Jimmy's bag from the boot and said, "How long are you here?"

"Just two days," replied Jimmy.

"Man, that's a long way for two days!" Laughed Andy.

"You need a lift tomorrow?"

"Yes, I have a meeting at the restaurant at 9am with the police."

"No problem, it's nearby, so I can pick you up say 8.50am?"

"That'll be good."

"Sorry Jimmy, but I've got a lot of worked booked for tonight, you ok if I don't hang around?"

"Of course."

"See you in the morning my friend," said Andy.

They embraced like brothers and Jimmy watched the old Austin pull out of the driveway.

He walked in past a small indoor pond in the reception. The place reminded him of the Government buildings he used to work in, columns reached up to white ceilings with their fans rotating. Leather and dark wood furniture decorated the lobby area.

Jimmy checked in and was shown to his room by a smart, polite young concierge in a crisp white shirt and chinos. He opened the door and Jimmy had to admit it, the room certainly had a wow factor. Everything was big. The bed, the seating area and a balcony overlooking the ocean.

"The mini bar is here and has a selection of spirits, wine and beer. If you need anything, just dial extension 2. I hope you enjoy your stay sir."

Jimmy tipped him three US dollars and then went downstairs. The dining room was like a film set from the 1940s, simply beautiful. After eating some grilled fish and listening to a very talented guitarist, Jimmy was asleep in his room by ten.

He awoke at 6am to the sound of the sea, a sound he loved. He walked out onto the balcony. The view over the tropical gardens was stunning, exactly how he'd imagined the Caribbean to be: blue sea, palm trees, sunshine glinting off the bobbing boats. A rainbow appeared as it had just stopped raining. It was certainly no mystery why Engels would want to come here! On the beach was a young Barbadian raking the sand. Jimmy smiled at the sight of early rising guests possessively planting their towels on whichever lounger they'd grabbed.

Jimmy showered and dressed into a blue lightweight linen suit and a white cotton shirt; he wanted to put his best foot forward. He sat at a table outside for breakfast and it was already twenty-eight degrees. At 8.50, Andy picked him up and they took the short drive to the meeting.

The gates of The Plantation Restaurant were already open. The building itself was a converted ex-mansion, built in a plantation style, hence the name, and only yards from the white sands that met the rippling sea. Parked out front was a white Land Rover with a tall Barbadian leaning against the front of the vehicle. The man's angular face was complemented by a pair of Ray-Bans. He was wearing the blue uniform of the Barbadian police and appeared pretty sure of himself as he threw his head back, exhaling cigarette smoke.

"Morning. I'm Jimmy Watson, Lloyd's, London."

"Well, morning, Mr Lloyd's of London."

The man slapped his big hand into Jimmy's. "My name is Chief Inspector Wade Anderson. Hope you're enjoying our beautiful island."

"I certainly am."

The inspector turned and, signaling to a wiry male sitting on the steps to the restaurant, said, "This is Kenny, he is the manager, who's kindly opened up for us."

"Nice to meet you, I appreciate your help."

Kenny nodded, pulled himself up and led them into the restaurant that was decorated very old-school Caribbean: white tablecloths on round tables, a large dark oak bar, over which hung low ceiling fans. It was a big area with beautiful views all around. Jimmy noticed the stingrays coming close to the shore. He guessed: *this is where the restaurant would throw out food waste into the water*. The place had been shut for nearly two weeks since Engels' death.

Kenny pointed to some double doors behind the bar.

"The kitchen is through there. Sad, you know man, he was a good guy."

Jimmy and the inspector entered a huge cooking and preparation area with stainless steel and timber work tops, multiple racks on the white-tiled wall. One was inscribed, "The Plantation." On the floor by a large oven was a black and brown stain, which Jimmy guessed were from where Engels had fallen. The paint on some of the cupboards had been burnt off with the flames. The big Barbadian policeman crouched down.

"As you can see, Mr Engels fell here, maybe drunk. His wife had come to meet him and was waiting near the front door when she heard his screams."

"Sounds bloody awful," said Jimmy.

He looked at the floor. The staining was fat that had melted off the burning body.

"Do you need to see anything else?"

Jimmy stood up and scanned the kitchen. "No, I think I'm all done."

"We found nothing suspicious, just seems a tragic accident," said Anderson.

As the two men reached the front door of the restaurant, Jimmy said, "I'd like to see Engels' body."

"Well, that will be difficult."

"Why?"

"It was cremated two days ago!"

"That was quick!"

"Mrs Engels wanted to get on with the burial as soon as possible. We had no reason to stop the ceremony, especially as he was semi-cremated already!" He gave Jimmy a faint smile.

"Is that some sort of fuckin' bad joke?"

The inspector started laughing out loud, "I thought you English were supposed to have a sense of humour." He laughed again.

"Can I get a copy of the post-mortem?"

"Yes of course, it still has to be typed up, so you'll have it in London on your return."

"I'd like to look inside Engels' flat."

"Sorry my friend, but our arrangement with Lloyd's was purely a courtesy on our part. We are not tour guides. My time doesn't extend to showing you around his home I'm afraid. Enjoy your day!"

The inspector outstretched his arm for a handshake. This was obviously Jimmy's cue to leave.

When Jimmy got outside, the day had got hotter. Andy was leaning up against his car.

"Any good Jimmy?"

"Looks pretty much as reported. Got drunk and then toasted himself! Any idea where Engels lived?"

"Yeah, not far from here. I dropped him off a few times. You wanna go there now?"

"If we could."

A few minutes later, Andy was turning down onto an unmade road to the side of an imposing building protected by high railings.

Number 2 Sandy Lane was formerly a grand residence built in the nineteen-thirties. It had been converted into apartments in the early seventies.

They walked around the back of the property to a large wooden gate, with a large deep step leading up from the beach. Fortunately, the sea was out just about enough for them to get up onto the step without getting wet. The gate was locked. Jimmy retrieved a small bunch of assorted keys from his jacket and on the third try, opened the gate. They followed a narrow path splitting two immaculate lawns which led to a set of French doors that were open. They made their way to the front lobby and saw on one of the brass letter boxes that Flat 2 on the second floor belonged to P. Engels. The two of them climbed some marble stairs into a whitewashed hallway. Engels apartment was at the end of the landing.

Using the same small bunch of keys, Jimmy entered the front door which led straight into a sunny beautiful lounge. The soft furnishings were all white, with hard furniture in dark wood contrasting beautifully. A set of double doors led onto a balcony.

There were two bedrooms, the first dominated by a four-poster bed with a voile curtain running around it. The wardrobes were full of only men's clothes.

The second bedroom had a more feminine décor with the wardrobes full of women's clothes. He had to admit the guy had taste. They searched, but the flat did not reveal any secrets.

As the two men left, the sea had come in and was lapping the back step, so they left via the front door.

"Looks all pretty normal Andy. I'll walk back. Come for dinner tonight, say 8pm at the hotel?"

"I'd like that!"

*

That night as they sat at the bar, Andy said, "You guessed yet why all the staff are looking at us?"

"Search me."

"They're not used to seeing a black guy this side of the bar, especially in a place like this!"

"And certainly not one that talks like Cliff Richard!" Jimmy joked.

"Fuck off man!" he laughed.

"Now that's not very Cliff, is it?"

Jimmy looked around and sure enough judging by the stares they were getting, Andy was right.

"Anyway, back to Engels, did you find out anything?"

"A bit of a player: likes the ladies; the sort of guy that would shag a palm tree if you let him. Likes a gamble, or should I say *liked* a gamble. His wife isn't seen out here that much, which I think suited him. Generally, pretty well liked, usually here for about four months of the year, December until end of March. No scandals as far as I could find out. It'll be a big loss to the area if the restaurant doesn't reopen."

Jimmy looked up. "Is there a casino on the Island?"

"No man, he'd be into private card games, high stakes and all that with some of his rich friends."

Jimmy looked at the menu.

"Well, what you having for dinner?"

For the next few hours, the pair reminisced about the old days. At around midnight, a very drunk Andy got up, but before he left, he said, "You know what Jimmy, you were the only guy in the army who never saw the colour of my skin. That meant a lot to me!"

Jimmy felt embarrassed. They bid farewell to each other, and Andy made his unsteady way to his car. As he did so Jimmy shouted,

"Don't get arrested, drink driving!" Andy held his hand up and got into the old Cambridge.

*

The next day, Jimmy stayed at the hotel enjoying the sun, the drink and the food. In the evening he walked into Holetown and drank at the aptly named Love Bar, where he was offered a choice of dope, sex and drink. He stuck with the drink and bravely wandered back to his hotel at around one in the morning, where at the Reception, a smiling beautiful girl asked him if he'd had a good evening.

"Lovely, thank you," and then he staggered to bed.

The following day, he woke up early around 6am. His body was telling him that it was 10am in the UK so it was time to get up. He showered and went down to breakfast. Sitting there like Billy No Mates, other guests gave him a knowing smile that said, *Ah, the poor bastard is on his own.*

Jimmy perched himself on a sun bed after breakfast, watching the pink, red, brown and lobster-coloured bodies go by in various shapes and sizes. He thought, *Why is it women that shouldn't be seen dead in a bikini wear one, and the ones that could, don't? And what's with all these fat bastards wearing white Speedos?*

After lunch Jimmy made his way to the front of the hotel and there was Andy waiting by the black Cambridge.

"You all set Jimmy?"

"All set Andy. Just wish my stay had been longer."

At the airport, Andy got Jimmy's bag out and handed it to him. "Come back soon Cap'n."

"Just might, Sergeant." He gave Andy a mock salute and made his way into the airport.

Jimmy landed in London at 6.30 am. He had managed to sleep a bit as thankfully, there were no crying babies.

Two hours later, Jimmy was staring out of the fourth-floor window at Lloyd's in Lime Street, watching the rain bounce off the pavement. Amanda's voice behind him said,

"She'll see you now."

Jimmy entered Ward's office. She signalled him to sit down, she was on the phone. On putting the receiver down, she looked across at Jimmy.

"Well, how'd it go? I bet the weather was better than here?"

"All good, seems to be what you said. Pretty much a tragic accident by all accounts." He then gave a full account of his trip.

"Well, we've got Engels' wife on the phone every day, asking about the insurance payout. She's like a bloody stalker! I need you to fly to Rome to ask a her a few questions which Amanda will give you to rehearse, and then we can make a final decision once we see that post-mortem."

"Lesley, I thought I was supposed to be getting experience for your fraud department, not becoming a blimmin' travel agent."

"Look Jimmy, it's all part of the job and I can't travel anyway. It's a bit of box ticking, but it has to be done. Amanda will make the arrangements again and it's £300 for one night in Rome. Is that so bad, eh?" She looked at him with questioning eyes.

Jimmy held his hands up in surrender. "Ok, if that's what you want, but I'm not so sure we are going to gain much by me slapping off to Rome."

She looked up, "Have a good trip!"

As he walked out into Amanda's office, she was obviously already taking instructions from Ward.

"Jimmy, are you at home after twelve, as I will call you with the flight details for tomorrow?"

"Yes, I'll be there."

"Just hang on while I type you some notes."

CHAPTER THREE

Nutted by Reality

Jimmy had last been in Rome in 1965. He'd spent two weeks in The Eternal City and had come across the fascination the Italian rich had with the Roman underworld. They'd befriend them, socialise with them and even go into business with them; but it was never an equal partnership, even though they'd kid themselves that it was. Many a time a family would find their whole livelihood had been taken away from under their noses.

It was midday as he came through the arrival doors at Ciampino airport, he could see what could only be described as a Barry Gibb lookalike holding up a placard reading, "J Wotson." *Near enough,* thought Jimmy.

"I'm Jimmy, from Lloyd's of London."

The Bee Gee of Rome smiled, "I'm Marco, from Napoli. Follow me."

Jimmy followed this hairy-chested vision in high-waisted tight white flares, black shirt and gold medallion, mincing his way to a parked gold Fiat 124. Jimmy had only just done up his seat belt as the car roared away, throwing him back in his brown velour seat. "Night Fever" blasted from the tape cassette.

"You like da Bee Gees?" asked the Italian.

"Yes, very good!"

When Jimmy had gone to prison in 1967, they were a pretty cheesy Australian trio; now they were the coolest men on the planet.

Marco turned the volume up and tapped the steering wheel to the music.

"You bin to Rome before?"

Jimmy had to shout, "Yes a long time ago."

"It's a bootafool city, yes?"

Jimmy nodded.

"Where you from?" said Marco.

"London."

"I gotta sister in London, Finsbury Park. 'Er 'usband got a pizza place, very bootafool."

"Smashing."

They drove at high speed while Marco constantly looked at himself in the rear-view mirror, flicking his hair. The journey into Rome was usually around thirty minutes, whereas Marco seemed to want to do it in twenty. Jimmy thought, *This guy could get us killed.*

"You always been a taxi man?" he called, above the noise of the engine.

"Me, nah, I used to be a fisherman wid my fader."

"You sure you weren't a fuckin' racing driver?"

He turned to Jimmy: "You, very funny man!"

"So I've been told."

They sped along the SS7 motorway, passing the Hippodrome, and then the Parco Degli Acquedotti, the site of the old Roman water systems. Marco turned onto the Appia Antica, passing the catacombs and through the ancient walls on the outskirts of the city. The Rome pine trees that decorate the skyline came into view. The car rumbled over the cobbles of central Rome and thumped up and down on narrow roads where you could reach out and literally touch the restaurant tables. Unlike London, the April air outside was warm.

The car stopped outside Hotel Raphael, the front of which was covered with ivy and vines, making it one of Rome's prettiest-looking hotels. It is situated by the Edicola Sacra, near the Piazza Navona. In front of the hotel was a raised terrace where a waiter was serving drinks. As Jimmy took out his small case from the boot, Marco handed him a card.

"Call me anytime."

"Sure…While thinking, "*There's no way I'm getting in a car again with that fucking madman.*

And with that, the speeding Bee Gee pulled away to the sound of "Jive Talkin'."

Jimmy entered a spacious marble Reception and checked in. His room was small, but nicely decorated. He sat on the bed and dialled Karen Engels' number.

"Mrs Engels, it's Jimmy Watson from Lloyd's, London. I was wondering if we could meet? We just have some loose ends to tie up, all very routine."

"Ah, your office called yesterday. Would you like to meet me in say, one hour? The address is 1779 Via Giuliana."

"See you then."

He could see from the map he'd been given, that it was around a twenty-minute walk, so he took time out and made his way to the bar first, and after a couple of much-needed Ichnusa beers, walked to the address.

Via Giuliana is a long road of flat-fronted nineteenth-century apartment buildings. It is one of central Rome's most desirable streets and has been home to many celebrities, the most famous being Audrey Hepburn who had married, not a fellow film star, but a humble dentist.

Jimmy found Engel's apartment block and buzzed the intercom which opened a metal gate, opening into a white hallway lined with various indoor plants. He climbed two flights of stone steps and arrived at Apartment 5 and pressed yet another buzzer. The door was opened by a woman of around forty years of age. She was attractive, tall with blonde blow-waved hair, Abba style. She was dressed expensively in black slacks topped with a red silk blouse. She wore no shoes.

"Oh, it's you," she said dismissively, as if his phone call hadn't happened.

She turned away from him and walked back along the hallway; he assumed he should follow her. The lounge was big and decorated in classic Italian style: varnished shutters, whitewashed walls, lots of pictures and too much antique furniture. She sat down on a cream settee, with what looked like a large whisky resting on its arm. She folded her left leg underneath her and placed her arms along the top of the couch. She didn't offer Jimmy a drink and he sat uncomfortably on a chair opposite her. He took out a packet of Muratti cigarettes and offered her one; she leant over and took it, and he lit it for her and then his own. She leaned back into the settee and looked at Jimmy.

"So, Mr Lloyd's of London, I hope you brought your cheque book!"

"That's not my department."

"Well, what is your department?"

"I'd like to ask a few questions."

"Well, ask away," she said exhaling smoke.

"I understand you were at the restaurant the night of your husband's accident?"

"Yes, it was around one in the morning. I'd gone to meet him; he sometimes liked to cook for himself late."

"Did you hear your husband's cries?"

"Yes, it was horrific. By the time I got to the kitchen, poor Peter was engulfed in flames. I tried to help him by throwing water over him but that seemed to make things worse. I called for an ambulance. They got there in around twenty minutes; it seemed like an eternity. By that time he was dead. I'll never forget those screams."

She buried her head in her hands and made a sobbing noise. To Jimmy, it was like watching a hammy actor.

"What do you think happened?"

She pulled her hands away and Jimmy could see no tears. Jimmy took out a small notebook.

"Peter always liked to drink, maybe he had too much that night, who knows?"

"Did you know your husband had only recently increased his life insurance cover?"

"No, I didn't." She drew hard on the cigarette, closing one of her eyes against the smoke.

"Did you know he was heavily in debt?"

"No."

"Did your husband have any enemies who might want to see him dead?"

She took a long stare at Jimmy.

"Listen, I don't like where this is going, I've only just lost my husband in a tragic accident."

Jimmy kept pressing.

"Do you think your husband was capable of suicide?"

"Don't be ridiculous, Peter had everything to live for."

"What was your relationship like?"

"Do I have to answer any more questions?"

"Only if you want to."

"In that case, this conversation is over. I suggest you go back to climbing on dustbins and taking dirty pictures or whatever it is you do. It's funny, the minute there's a claim, you fuckin' insurance arseholes want to find a loophole."

She marched to the front door and swung it wide open, looking down at the floor.

"I think you'd better go."

Jimmy stood up and put the notebook away.

"Well, thank you for your help."

"Just send the fucking cheque!"

As Jimmy walked back to his hotel he thought about their conversation. *She sure was desperate for the money, but it didn't mean her husband hadn't died the way she'd described. Maybe he was looking for something that wasn't there!*

He passed a beautiful fountain in a small side street. It reminded him of what a guide had once told him: "*Rome is like an open-air museum,*" and they were right. Everywhere you turned, there was something to look at.

When he arrived back at the hotel, before handing Jimmy his key, the male receptionist said, "There's a gentleman waiting to see you."

Jimmy turned, and sitting by the window was a large muscular male in a black suit. He had a bald, shiny bullet-head with sunglasses perched on top of it. He pulled himself up out of the chair unsteadily, in the way muscle-bound men tend to.

"Mr Jimmy Watson, Nicky Taylor sends his regards and asks you come with me as he has some helpful information for you." He had what Jimmy recognised as a drawling New York accent.

Jimmy had to think who Nicky Taylor was. *Of course*, the penny dropped. He'd known him back in London as Micky Shit-Tats. For years, Jimmy always thought that he was Greek, until one drunken night, it was pointed out that his last name was in fact Taylor, but the "Shit-Tats" referred to some really bad tattoos he'd acquired years before in Soho. The "Nicky" came out as Micky and the Mandarin letters tattooed on his chest, didn't read "I'm a Soldier", but "I'm a Wanker". No doubt the joking tattooist had got a hiding when Nicky got a translation.

Shit-Tats was a villain and not a bright one at that. He'd operated as an enforcer through the gangster heydays of the sixties. He liked to rough people up, he was old-school muscle, worked the doors of night clubs; dealt drugs, all the usual low-life stuff.

Now, Nicky loved all things Italian: the fashions, the cars, and of course, Italian women. He got lucky at the age of twenty-four in 1962, when he met and married Maria Fontana, daughter of one of the Fontana brothers, Frankie Fontana, (also known as Palermo Frankie). Frankie's brother Alfonso became a victim in the Setty murders in the 1950s, and his body parts, probably dumped from a light aircraft, were found in different places all over Canvey Island. Fontana had a reputation that he would cut or kill anyone who tried to compete with him in business, be it legal or otherwise. During the 'sixties and 'seventies, Frankie had made a fortune running sex shops in Soho, then known as "The Jungle". Now he'd moved into waste disposal and in particular, hospital waste contracts, that were supposed to be dealt with using specialist chemicals but were dumped out at sea or exported in shipping containers to rot on the side of the docks in Brazil or wherever.

As for Shit-Tats, in 1974 things had got a little hot for him in London and his father-in-law had grown tired of having to bail out his troublesome son-in-law. Shit-Tats had learnt, if you control the doors to a club, you control the drugs, but he was making too many waves for the family. (His own father had come a cropper with Fontana the year before). For the sake of his daughter, Fontana orchestrated a move to Rome for Micky, where he would work for the family as a money lender and launderer. Once there, he'd kept the local villains happy with regular payments, but the real brains behind the operation was his wife, Maria, who ran a bar as a front. He still provided the brawn, especially when it came to dealing with late payers. He still enjoyed administering "a bit of a lesson."

Jimmy looked at the big man. *How the hell did Shit-Tats know he was in Rome and what was this helpful information? There was only one way to find out.*

"Ok, lead the way."

Parked outside the hotel was a silver 1963 Maserati Quattroporte. Jimmy got in the passenger side. The big man got in and started the big V8 saloon. The leather seats were hot from the sun. The car throbbed through the narrow streets for ten minutes, pulling up in Campo dei Fiori.

"Over there," said Bullet-Head, pointing a sausage-like finger.

Jimmy could see Micky, who was sitting on the terrace of "Nicky's" restaurant and bar. It was situated on a corner, opposite a square occupied by market stalls selling fruit and veg and Roman souvenirs. Traders called out to tourists, while waiters stood in front of their restaurants, displaying their menus, trying to lure customers in. At the centre of the square was a statue of Giordino Bruno, looking down on everyone.

Shit-Tats wore a black shirt and trousers, and as Jimmy sat down, he tried not to smile, as Shit-Tats was wearing the worst toupée he had ever seen. It was styled in a sort of quiff from Elvis's fat period. (Presley had died the previous August). Jimmy stared for a moment and thought, *Why is it wig-wearers kid themselves nobody notices they are walking around with a Shredded Wheat on their head?*

"Micky, great to see you."

"It's Nicky, not Micky."

"Sorry, *Nicky*," Jimmy said, repeating the name slowly.

Jimmy shook Shit-Tats' sweaty fat hand, who didn't get up. In front of him on the table was a large bottle of Peroni. He called to one of the waiters, "Another one of these for my friend."

Jimmy sat down.

"Long time no see, Nicky."

"Heard you were banged up, son."

"I was, came out last year."

Shit-Tats' face looked flushed and shiny. He was sweating profusely with sweat rings under his shirt armpits. *He must be hot under that fuckin' rug*, thought Jimmy.

"Looks like you're doin' alright these days; this your pace?" Said Jimmy.

"The wife's."

"You enjoying life here, Nicky?"

"In this town, I don't 'ave to put up with fuckin' East End comedians like you anymore. Still a funny boy, are yah?"

"Not so much these days. Nothing to laugh about."

"What you need to understand, son, that in this city, I'm a respected businessman. My world 'as moved on a lot since we were knocking about in the clubs."

"Baldy over there tells me you have some information read for me?" Said Jimmy, leaning forward.

"Our mutual friend Engels has been a naughty boy and I 'eard you was asking about 'im."

Jimmy nodded and said, "I take it you've been talking to the not so merry widow who I saw this morning?"

"Could be. Anyway, Peter was a gambler and like all these mugs do, borrowed a lot of dough off just about anyone he could. So, he comes knocking on my door. So, what happens? I'll tell yah. He don't pay me back the money 'I've lent 'im, and I'm now just waiting for his missus to get the insurance money, so she can settle me up, but you're asking awkward questions that could well jeopardise my payout."

Jimmy was sure the wig had moved, and found himself looking to Shit-Tats' head, who continued, "Now, think how upset I'm gonna be not to get my money. You don't want to upset your old pal, do yah Jimmy?"

"Look Nicky, I'm just doing a job, tying up some loose ends for the insurance company, that's all."

"I don't think you're listening to me. I'm not some fuckin' mug loose end. Now what you're gonna do, is go back to your hotel, get your stuff and fuck off on the first plane back to London. Do you understand?"

Jimmy got up.

"I think you've been watching too many gangster films mate."

Jimmy started to walk away.

"Where you fuckin' goin'? I'm not finished with you yet."

"Micky, Nicky, Wiggy or whatever your fuckin' name is these days, I'm going back to my hotel, but I ain't flying anywhere until I get some answers."

As Jimmy walked away, he knew the reality was that this was not going to be a simple little job like Lesley had told him. Shit-Tats waved Bullet-Head to come over to him.

On Jimmy's part it was all bravado. He was going home the next day anyway and if he was honest, he couldn't think of any questions that could be answered in Rome anyway!

CHAPTER FOUR

Airport

Back at his hotel, Jimmy closed his eyes for a while, got changed and went down to the bar, drowning his doubts in Scotch. (He was still promising himself to cut down on the booze). After what he'd heard from Shit-Tats that morning, he was convinced that Peter Engels must have been murdered and that his wife must be in on it, and maybe Shit-Tats too. The two of them obviously had something friendly going on. Until being summoned by dear old Nicky Taylor, he'd been ready to report back to Lesley that he had found nothing suspicious.

At around 8.30, a barman with an exotic moustache, that wouldn't have looked out of place in a porn film, leant on the bar.

"You fancy going somewhere where there's plenty of girls and a bit of fun?"

He wobbled his head in a you-know-what-I-mean way.

Jimmy knocked back his drink.

"As it happens, I wouldn't mind a bit of fun."

The barman leaned even closer as if he was about to tell Jimmy some sort of big secret.

"There's two nightclubs I can recommend. Jackie O's, or a place called The Piper Club. See the concierge over there? He will call you a cab."

He gave Jimmy a knowing wink.

That sounds interesting, thought Jimmy, and slid a note across the bar.

Thirty minutes later, he got out of a cab on the Via Tagliamento, on the Solano-Coppede border, one of Rome's more exclusive suburbs. The Piper Club had a double set of doors leading down past two doormen into a basement club. Beyond the doors, the space opened out, where there were around two hundred diners seated. The place was rocking. A beautiful mixed-race girl in a cocktail dress had just started her set. He sat at the bar, watching her sing standards such as "Love for Sale" and "Fly Me to the Moon". Looking around, it seemed that to get in, it was compulsory that the men had to be old, but women had to be young. A line of topless girls came on stage and danced to "You're The One That I Want." For the next few hours, he sat at the bar, chatting drinking, smoking, and people-watching.

It must have been just after 1am when he heard a Cockney girl's voice order a drink. He turned; it was one of the dancers. She was around five foot two, petite, with short dark hair. She had long dancer's legs; she was perfectly proportioned.

"I enjoyed your show," he said.

"No, you enjoyed looking at my tits!"

Jimmy put his hands up. "Guilty as charged! You lived in Rome long?"

"About a year."

"What got you into topless work then?"

"What are you, me fuckin' dad?"

"Sorry, it was a stupid question."

She sat up on a stool.

"Well, if you must know, I was in the chorus line at the back not earning much, but once I found out you get double pay if you're happy to get yah tits out and get down the front, I was straight in. After all, I'm not going to run into anyone I know from home around here."

"I like your logic. Can I buy you that drink you've just ordered?"

"Why not? My name's Lucy. You on holiday?"

"Work. I'm in insurance."

"Sounds exciting."

"I think you're taking the piss!"

She knocked back her Bacardi and Coke in one. "I needed that!"

From behind her, another English girl, also from the topless routine, came over. "Lucy, our lift's here."

Lucy stood, smiling, and held her hand out, waiting for him to speak.

"The name's Jimmy."

"Well, it was nice to meet you, Jimmy." As she walked away, she turned and said, "Oh, and thanks for the drink. Come see us another night."

She raised her hand, and the two girls left. He smiled to himself and decided he too may as well call it a day.

Outside, he got into a cab but the mixture of fresh air and too much alcohol made him lightheaded. After around fifteen minutes, he didn't feel great, so decided to get out at Ponte Vittorio Emanuel and walk the rest of the way to the hotel. He crossed the bridge onto a street that was dimly lit from the old cast-iron lamps spaced out along the apartment fronts.

As he walked up Via Dei Coranari, he was suddenly caught in the beam of the big headlights of Bullet-Head's Maserati. He knew he wasn't being followed for just a friendly chat. Jimmy quickened his pace and then broke into a run. Bullet-Head was catching up fast. As Jimmy reached a crossroads where a restaurant was just closing up, a couple were kissing passionately whilst standing next to an old Vespa scooter, which had its engine running. Jimmy barged them out of the way and jumped onto the saddle.

"Sorry mate," he shouted as he throttled the engine and sped off down the street. The young Italian shouted expletives at him. Heavy rain had started to fall. Jimmy weaved around bins, badly-parked cars, and courting couples who stood back as he steered his way unsteadily. Outside his hotel he abandoned the scooter and hurriedly made his way through the main doors. The night duty receptionist smiled and passed him his room key. "*Buona notte*," she said, as he quickly grabbed it and made his way to the lift.

In his room, he dug out the card of Marco the taxi driver and rang him.

"'Ello," Marco said sleepily.

"Marco, it's Jimmy Watson. I need your help – I need to get out of Rome tonight, I've got trouble. Can you get me to the airport as soon as possible, I need you here as soon as!"

"Fuckin' hell Jimmy, do you know what time it is?"

"It's serious Marco."

"Ok, ok, I'll bring me brudder."

"Bring your fuckin' mum if you like but just get here. I'll meet you out front."

Still rain-soaked, he quickly packed and was just zipping his bag up when he heard two car doors slam. He looked out between the blinds and could see the big Maserati parked outside. Bullet-Head and a young companion had just got out of the car. He quickly made his way down the stairs of the hotel and peered through a small window in the exit door at the bottom. The young guy was guarding the front entrance, Bullet-Head had obviously gone up in the lift. Jimmy pressed the bar on the fire escape door that led onto Vicolo della Pace, but it was jammed. He returned to looking through the door.

Two minutes later, he heard "Tragedy" blasting from the gold Fiat as it pulled up. Bullet-Head's man looked over his shoulder to see where the music was coming from. As he did so, Jimmy burst through the door and swung his bag, catching him on the side of the head, knocking him back over an umbrella stand, leaving him splayed by the front window.

Jimmy ran out and scrambled into the back of Marco's car. As the car sped away Marco shouted, "Meet ma brudder, Paolo."

He reached over from the front passenger seat and shook Jimmy's hand.

Fuck me, another Bee Gee lookalike, thought Jimmy.

The car was doing around sixty KPH, which felt more like a hundred, as it shifted over the uneven cobbled streets. A fox was caught in the headlights and then darted into the darkness.

After ten minutes, they pulled onto the Via Appia Nuova, but almost immediately as they did so, they could see the Maserati behind them. The Fiat was no match for the big V8, which was closing in fast behind them. Paolo reached down in front of him and before Jimmy could say anything, Paolo was hanging out of the window with an assault rifle. A burst of fire rang out. At first the Maserati kept pace, then it moved sideways and suddenly the lights were rolling as it crashed and slid on its roof.

Jimmy leant forward.

"What the fuck!"

"Calm down Jimmy, if those guys had caught us, we'd be dead," said Marco.

His brother said something in Italian and laughed.

"Just out of interest, Paolo, what do you do for a living?" asked Jimmy.

"Me? Security."

Marco and Paolo smiled at each other, and both started laughing again. Jimmy realised that Marco was no ordinary taxi driver, and God knows who his brother worked for, but it wasn't the sort of security Woolworths employed.

They stopped at Terminal One at Ciampino airport. Jimmy reached over the front seats and handed Marco 200 dollars he had left over from Barbados.

"Listen, I appreciate what you two did for me back there."

"Anytime my friend. When in Rome!" The brothers laughed hysterically again.

"Nights on Broadway" rang out as their car pulled away. If everything wasn't so serious, it would have been funny.

Apart from a few cleaners, the airport was virtually deserted. The first flight to London was at 7am; it was only 3.30am, so Jimmy had to wait until 6am to buy a ticket back to Heathrow. Once in the Departures lounge, he felt safe from Shit-Tats' reach.

It was clear that old Micky had become a major player in Rome and Jimmy had underestimated him. Shit-Tats' car was wrecked and two of his men were either injured or dead; Jimmy knew this was only the start of the real trouble.

*

Just after 8am, he touched down in London and rang Ward's PA.

"Oh, hi Jimmy, we thought you were back later."

"It's vital I see Lesley; is she in?"

"She's at a conference at Gleneagles, but I'm sure she will want to see you if it's that urgent?"

"It is."

"Where are you now?"

"I'm at Heathrow."

"One second… I'm looking at Teletext and I can see there's a flight to Edinburgh at 10am. If you're up for it, I will arrange for a pickup at Edinburgh and let Lesley know you'll be at the hotel around 12.30pm."

CHAPTER FIVE

Mystery Dance

Four and a half hours later, Jimmy climbed into the Land Rover Defender that had been sent for him. The drive to Gleneagles took around an hour. The day was bright but cold.

Jimmy and the driver made small talk about the weather, golf, the state of Scottish football, and he listened to the man's love of fishing, a subject Jimmy knew nothing about. The Land Rover pulled in between the main gates, and they passed the practice course and then the Queen's Course and the clubhouse. They turned right and then reached the roundabout that led directly down the driveway to Gleneagles Hotel itself, a magnificent stone-coloured twentieth-century building. In the 1930s, with its three golf courses, it was a regular feature on the high-society circuit, where you would sail at Cowes, play polo at Deauville, golf, and then grouse shoot at "Glenny."

Parked outside the main building was an old green Rolls Royce Silver Ghost, obviously positioned there for the tourist photo opportunities.

Jimmy got out and was greeted at the entrance by a middle-aged kilt-wearing commissioner. Jimmy looked back over towards the course. It was thirteen years since he'd been invited to play here, where he'd seen the likes of Sean Connery, Bruce Forsyth and Ronnie Corbett playing in pro-ams. Those were the days when Jimmy was in his pomp. How times had changed for him.

Inside, he walked past a log fire on his left, up to the reception in what was certainly an impressive lobby. A stout woman in her forties, wearing tweeds, addressed him.

"Good afternoon and welcome to Gleneagles Sir. Are you staying with us?"

"Yes, just for one night. My name is Watson."

She looked for his name on the reservations list.

"You've stayed with us before?"

"Yes, a long time ago."

"Well, it's good to have you back. Ah yes, you're in Room 305, billed to Lloyd's Insurance. Is that correct?"

"Yes."

"Do you need a hand with your luggage?"

"I'm fine, I travel light." She looked over the desk and could see Jimmy's overnight bag. She then scanned the rest of him standing there in creased Chinos, shirt and leather jacket. He felt somewhat intimidated.

"Would you happen to know where Miss Lesley Ward is? I'm due to meet her," he said.

Another lady on the desk joined the conversation.

"Yes, she was here a little earlier and said to direct you to the Century Bar. It's just behind you on the left."

The Century Bar is a large *art deco* room with a square-shaped bar situated in the centre, nicely decorated with plush velvet and sateens, echoing a bygone era. As he entered, he could see Ward by one of the large windows with a large red wine in one hand and a cigarette in the other. She was wearing a Harris Tweed shooting jacket with a matching kilt. She fitted in very comfortably in these surroundings. He noticed the plaster on her leg was gone. On seeing Jimmy, her face lit up.

"Aha, the wanderer returns. So, what's so urgent that we have to fly you all the way up here?"

He recounted what had happened in Rome, being interrupted once when a waiter asked him what he wanted to drink.

Ward peered at Jimmy over her glasses through the cigarette smoke.

"Well, it all sounds like you could be onto something. What do you need to investigate it further?"

"Lesley, I have no experience in this sort of thing. Maybe it's time to bring somebody else in?"

"Nonsense, you've done pretty well so far. Look, there's a lot of money at stake here, so tell me what you need, expenses-wise."

After twenty minutes and some small talk, they'd agreed £600 per week for Jimmy to continue, and £50 per day for anyone he brought in, plus expenses. Ward agreed to have some money transferred in advance to Jimmy, who had decided not to stay the night. He caught the nine o'clock flight back to London.

At almost midnight, exhausted, he climbed the stairs of his apartment block. As he arrived at his flat, he could see all the lights were off; he was sure he'd left some on. He slowly turned the door key, and as he walked softly into the lounge, there was a noise in the bathroom. He went to the kitchen and pulled out a large carving knife. He flicked the main lounge light switch, but nothing came on. In the dark, he waited by the bathroom door but as it opened, his assailant was too quick. A kick caught him, he dropped the knife and staggered backwards, clutching his manhood. The light from the bathroom glowed.

"Jimmy?"

Standing there with a towel wrapped around her, through watering eyes he could just make out his sister, Alison.

"What the fuck are you doin' here?" She screamed.

"I fuckin' live here," he groaned, "why are all the lights out?"

"I think the bulb's gone in the lounge and I turned the others off! As for why I'm here, well I've left Stan, and Dad said you were away and I could stay here."

"Sounds like Dad," he said sarcastically.

"I'll get you a cuppa, love, you're looking a bit white. Do you want me to rub something on them?"

"Alison, do you know how weird that sounds?"

After a few minutes Jimmy had composed himself.

"So how is the old man?"

"Still got the same bad habits, couldn't live wiv 'im for long."

They both laughed.

"Oh God, he's such a silly sod!"His sister cackled.

"Anyway, how come you finally decided to leave Stan?"

"Well, as you know I was doing work from home, so I takes some sewing in from a new bloke. He starts dropping off more and more stuff, having a cup a tea, a smoke, a chat and we get on really well. He then suggests that rather than staying indoors, would I take on a full-time job and manage a group of machinists in New Road. Well, I 'aven't worked outside the home for years, but I says 'yes', but Stan don't like me leaving the flat. So, after I've done it for a couple of weeks, he tells me to chuck the job in. I tells him 'no', and the bastard slaps me like he used to in the old days. I picked me handbag up and walked out. I 'ain't never goin' back."

"Well, good for you. Does your fella know you've left Stan?"

"He's not my fella," she grinned, "well, not yet!"

Jimmy had to smile, for this was like Alison from years ago. She'd coloured her hair since he'd last seen her and seemed to have her spark back.

"I will get some money out in the morning, so you can get some clothes and stuff. Look, stay here as long as you want," he smiled.

"Ah thanks Jim. It will be nice to spend some time with me little brother anyway. What do you want for dinner tomorrow night?"

"I think we'll celebrate. Where would you like to go? He said."

"Pie and mash would be lovely!"

"Always said you were a classy bird!"

She laughed.

*

The next morning, Alison had left early for work, looking excited. Jimmy suspected that fabric wasn't the only thing that was getting laid on the cutting table.

An hour later, Jimmy was sitting opposite Amanda at Lloyd's. She looked up and handed the post-mortem on Engels to him.

"The long-awaited PM for you!"

"Ok if I sit here and read it?"

"Sure, shall I get you a coffee?"

"Tea please, if that's ok, no sugar."

Jimmy sat on a slippery vinyl-covered two-seater couch and started reading. The pathologist who'd signed off the report was from the French speaking island of St Martin.

Height 1.8 metres, weight 69 kilos. There followed a long detail of the burn injuries, high alcohol levels, but nothing else seemed particularly unusual until he reached the last paragraph: *Individual in advanced stages of cancer.* Then another word leapt off the page: *Heroin. Cause of death, heart attack caused by trauma.*

Jimmy looked up at Amanda.

"Tell me: to increase his life cover, would Engels have to have had a medical?"

"Of course, especially as it was substantial."

"Could I see Peter Engels' medical records?"

Amanda picked up the phone.

"Could you bring up the file on Peter Engels please."

After a few minutes, a young man around eighteen years of age with a bad complexion, and looking very nervous in his new suit, brought two folders in, and handed them to Amanda. With a stammer he said,

"Th... the files you asked for Miss," as if he was still at school.

Jimmy then read through Engels' medical.

Height, 6ft 2in, weight 12 stone. There were blood test results but nothing showing cancer and no sign of drug use.

"Amanda, do you think I could see the doctor who did this medical, today?"

"I'll try – but you know what it's like trying to see a doctor at short notice!"

She picked up the phone and he listened to her argue with the doctor's receptionist, finally getting a window of fifteen minutes at midday.

Wimpole Street in the West End of London, runs parallel with Harley Street. Like most doctors' rooms in London, Number 89 was originally a grand house that had now been split up into three doctors' practices. The receptionist pointed Jimmy to a small waiting room. After around ten minutes, an elderly head showed itself around the door.

"I'm Doctor Adrian Harris, please follow me."

Jimmy followed the bow-legged septuagenarian down a narrow hallway back to his office. Both men sat down either side of a cluttered desk.

"I understand you have some questions about the medical report on Peter Engels?"

"Yes, I'm hoping you can help."

Jimmy passed the file over to the doctor.

"This is his post-mortem. I'm puzzled as it says Engels was in an advanced stage of cancer, when six months ago your medical showed nothing."

"Impossible, the blood tests would've picked up any signs of cancer."

The doctor started reading. "Christ, he'd taken enough heroin to kill five people, never mind himself. He would have suffered hypoxia, which means the amount of oxygen reaching the brain would have been massively decreased, which would have sent Peter into seizure and then no doubt a coma. Typically, he would have had blue lips and fingernails and clammy skin. I see the coroner in Barbados says he died of a heart attack caused by trauma due to burns, but I'd say he may have been already dead by the time he hit the floor."

"Could he have injected that amount of heroin himself?"

"Not likely. You've seen those scenes of addicts dead with the needles still in their arm?"

Jimmy nodded.

"Well, that's where they pass out and fail to inject the rest. I'd say someone else injected a dose this large into Peter. Were any needles found in or around the body?"

"Not to my knowledge."

Jimmy sat in silence as Harris read on.

"There's something not right here. It gives Engels' height as 1.8 metres, that's about 5ft 11ins. Peter was a 6ft 2ins man."

Jimmy was embarrassed, as he hadn't converted the metric measurements to feet and inches, so had missed this glaring fact.

"Could that be down to being burnt badly?"

"My friend, you don't lose three inches in height, even in a seriously hot fire, the skeleton will be the same height, it doesn't shrink. I'd say this is someone else's body."

"Are you sure?"

"Absolutely!"

The doctor looked at the grizzly photographs in the file and scanned the report.

"Anything else, Mr...?"

"Watson, Jimmy Watson. You've been very helpful Doctor, I appreciate your time at such short notice."

The doctor looked at him with disdain. Jimmy shook the doctor's hand, took back the report and left. *So, who the hell died in that kitchen?*

Walking across into Regent Street, he found a call box.

If Engels is alive, then where is he? He decided he needed to find out more about the man's past, which might give him a lead. He rang Amanda.

"Jimmy, how'd it go?" She asked.

"Very interesting. I'll tell you when I see you. Listen, do you have any details on Engels' first wife?"

"One moment, there was another file that lad brought up with the medical."

She read the ex-wife's details over the phone to him.

He rang the number he'd been given and arranged to meet her within the hour.

CHAPTER SIX

Grey Cortina

A taxi dropped Jimmy off at the top of Beak Street and he walked into Carnaby Street. It was alive with young punk rockers parading in their bondage wear, ripped jeans and Mohican haircuts.

The Coffee Express just off Carnaby Street in Ganton Street, was not the sort of establishment where Jimmy would have expected to find Engels' ex. After all, not long ago, she was a partner in a successful Mayfair restaurant, meeting and greeting the rich and famous.

It was three o'clock and the seating area of the café had around fourteen tables, in the corner of which some young guys were eating. A juke box played "Tommy Gun," by the Clash. The smell of cooked fat hung in the air.

Behind the counter were two women in their mid-forties. One had black scraped-back hair with a severe-looking, heavily made-up face; the other was a redhead and attractive, Jimmy hoped this would be

Engel's ex-wife. He approached and looked over a tall glass counter that contained various cakes and buns.

"Which one of you lovely ladies is Karen?"

The black-haired woman turned to the redhead.

"I think this bullshitter is for you."

Karen Engels, on her tiptoes, looked over the cabinet. "You Jimmy?"

"Yes, we spoke earlier."

"Come upstairs."

He followed her up a narrow staircase. She opened one of the doors and led him into a lounge, the front window of which, looked out onto a sign reading: "Massage Parlour."

"As you can see, my neighbours are somewhat colourful! Tea?"

"Yes please."

She went into a small galley kitchen.

"Ok if I take a seat?" said Jimmy.

"Carry on."

That same greasy smell of the caff she had probably become immune to, permeated throughout the flat. It reminded Jimmy, that as a kid, his mums' clothes would have that same lingering smell when she came home from her job in the local chippy.

Jimmy looked around the room. It was dated, with an electric imitation log fire covering the original fireplace. Various old photographs hung on the walls, several of which were of her and the woman downstairs in their younger days. Another showed a well-dressed middle-aged couple walking in what looked like Regent Street in the 1940s, who he guessed were her parents.

She came out of the kitchen and he noticed her hand tremored as she handed him a tea in a dainty china cup, a digestive biscuit resting in the saucer. She sat down opposite Jimmy.

"So, you want to speak to me about Peter?"

"First of all, I'm sorry for your loss."

"Thank you, but he's a bastard – or was! Still, I have to admit, I did shed a little tear for him."

Jimmy thought for a second, *this is going to be interesting.*

"Could you give me some background on Peter? I'm trying to understand what he was like."

She looked up at the ceiling for a few seconds and her eyes glazed over. He could see she was trying to compose herself.

"I met Peter when I was twenty-seven and he was only twenty-two, he'd just arrived from Glasgow. I was managing a restaurant in Wells Street, not far from here, and he started as one of the trainee chefs. He'd had a tough upbringing and had been involved with some bad stuff, but left Scotland and came to London.

"He was pretty rough around the edges but was a real talent and I liked him. After a while, we got together and for a few years it was good. When the head chef left The Star in Brewer Street, I recommended Peter. In those days, he was always keen to learn. He did well and after three years we married and soon set up our own restaurant.

As time went on, things changed. We were making great money, but he got pretty big-headed and started referring to himself in the third person. Things like, *Peter Engels doesn't take no for an answer. Peter Engels this, Peter Engels that.* He started to stay out all night sometimes, doing recreational drugs, and he loved to gamble and neither were ever my thing. I put up with a lot, but when I caught him stuck between the legs of a so-called friend of mine, that was it. To rub my face in it even more, her name was also Karen.

Unfortunately, I took the whole situation very badly and I'm embarrassed to admit, I went to pieces. It's been seven long years since we split. I ended up living with my dad here above the caff, and when he passed away, he left this place to me and my sister. That was her downstairs."

"You live here now?"

"Yes, back to our roots you could say, the customers are young, most are nice, and it pays the bills."

"How did you hear of Peter's death?"

"I still keep in touch with a few of our old friends, news like this travels fast."

"Is he the sort of man who could take his own life?"

"Anything's possible with Peter."

"Tell me, did he have many friends?"

"Peter was always picking up people who think they are his new best friend. Usually, they were someone who he'd brought into some get-rich-quick scheme, and when it goes wrong, which it often did, they'd be hurt but for some reason they still wanted to be his friend, but then he'd discard them. I saw it many times."

"When did you last see him?"

"At a funeral, two years ago."

"Has he many enemies?"

"Not really."

Jimmy put the cup down on a coffee table that was covered with cookery books and magazines. He stood up to leave.

"Just out of interest, why did you not change back to your maiden name after you divorced?"

She gave an uncomfortable smile. "We never got round to divorcing."

Jimmy stood up.

"Well Karen, you've been very helpful."

He shook her hand awkwardly.

He sensed she still had an affection for her ex-husband and for the life they had once had.

Back outside, Jimmy looked up along Carnaby Street. He remembered how this place had looked only eleven years ago, full of mods and hippies. Now the looked tacky and run-down.

He made his way to a call box and rang Lesley Ward's number.

"I hear you've been off to see the first wife!" Were Ward's first words.

"Yes. Just out of interest, can you dig out his will and tell me how the clause for the beneficiary is worded?"

"I've got the file on my desk, one second... Right, it reads: *'The beneficiary on the death of Mr Peter Engels...* blah, blah, oh here it is... *Mrs Karen Engels.'* All straightforward really."

"Well, it's not if you never divorced your first wife, who happens to be the Karen Engels I've just visited, and not "wife number two". She might be calling herself Karen Engels but unless he's a bigamist, which I doubt, they never married."

"Oh Christ, what a mess. Can you imagine what will happen when she finds out?" Said Ward.

"I'm thinking, shit and fan!"

"We'll check he's not a bigamist, just to be on the safe side."

Jimmy was already thinking of something much worse. *What will happen when Shit-Tats finds out?*

He continued: "I'm wondering why Engels would leave the money to his first wife? He doesn't sound like the sort of guy that would feel guilty about leaving her, so she could well be in on it. If she is, she must've gone to RADA, as she just gave quite a performance! She said anything is possible when I asked her if Engels could commit suicide. But the more I learn of him, I just don't buy it. After meeting that doctor, I'm convinced Peter Engels is alive."

"What do you want to do?"

"I've got a few things to sort out, let's speak tomorrow."

He put the phone down.

After waving down a cab, Jimmy arrived in Stratford at an old run down garage forecourt, nearly an hour later. It was just getting dark, but there was Dave McKenzie, known behind his back as Talk-Bollocks. He was out the front, wiping the windscreen of an old Morris Traveller. Jimmy had known him since school and he was the ultimate ducker-and-diver and a compulsive liar, which made him the perfect car salesman. He knew all the local gossip and was good at spreading it too.

"How's things, Davey?"

McKenzie turned and with a look of surprise, said,

"Fuck me, 'ow long's it been then?'

"Ten years."

He shook Jimmy's hand hard and held his arm affectionately.

"Last I 'eard of you was when your old man said you were in Switzerland with some bird, and you needed to sell your E-Type. Personally, I woulda kept the jam jar!"*

"I'm beginning to think that too! I suppose you sold it?"

"A punter bought it the next day."

"Well, I need a motor to smoke around in for about a monkey."*

"You ain't gonna get much for that, Jimmy, but I do 'ave something. Follow me."

They walked to the back of the forecourt.

"'Ere we are my son, Dagenham's finest. 1970 Ford Cortina 1600E in silver grey, whiplash aerial, racing trim, just like Tom Robinson says in the song. Wood and leather interior, tuned engine, lowered suspension, every schoolboy's fuckin' dream car. Came in yesterday, owner just got banged up for five years."

"Do I look like a fuckin' schoolboy?"

"Yours is a schoolboy's budget, my son."

"You got anything else?"

"Got a '69 Jag for eight hundred quid."

"I'll take the Cortina."

"Wise choice."

After doing some paperwork and parting with £500, Jimmy pulled onto the London Road heading towards Aldgate. The Ford was no E-Type but was a plucky little car. But the whiplash aerial and green stick-on sun visor with *Gary and Sharon* on it would have to go!

He parked up near his flat and as he entered, he saw his sister was on the settee with her knees wrapped underneath her; she looked as if she'd been crying a while. Her black eye-liner had run down her face which was reddened on one side, and one of her eyes looked bloodshot.

"Alison, what happened?" He delicately lifted her chin. She looked up, tearful.

"Jimmy, it was awful, some bloke came, I recognised 'im from years ago. 'E 'ad a big lump of a Yank geezer wiv 'im. He asked for you, but when I said you was out, the Yank slapped me. They looked in all the rooms and said there's more to come, whatever that means. You in some sorta' trouble?"

"I could be, be for all the right reasons for a change."

"The geezer I knew from when we was kids, but 'e had a stupid fuckin' syrup on is 'ead."

"You'd know him as the doorman from the Two Puddings."

"That's 'im!"

"I'm so sorry this has happened Alison, I think it would be safer to stay with the old man."

He drove her to their dad's house, a two-up two-down reminiscent of the sort of house all his friends were brought up in.

The three of them sat round the kitchen table. Jimmy told them what had happened since his meeting with Ward at The Ritz. His dad stared down at his cup, stirring his tea.

"Well Jimmy, trouble seems to follow you about, son."

"I'm in the middle of a shit storm I can't get out of Dad!"

"What you gonna do?"

"Remember Brian Lowe?"

"Another fuckin' headcase," he said in disgust.

"Well, I'm gonna see if he can help."

"Jimmy, when you came out of the nick, I thought you'd left all this nonsense behind."

"So did I!"

The three of them sat in silence.

Jimmy looked up. "Well, I'll be off then."

Alison, who had sat in shocked silence, leaned over and gave him a motherly hug.

"You be careful."

*

At 8pm, Jimmy arrived at the Community Gym in Canning Town. It was situated just off Prince Regents Lane in an old Methodist Hall. As he entered, the smell of sweat was quite overpowering. The familiar sound of bags being punched, boxers sparring and sniffing, brought long-forgotten memories back to him. As a kid he'd boxed a bit, but without success. Two young lads were arguing, while others were skipping or using weights. A few guys, some black, some white, hung around just watching.

Jimmy said to one of them, "Is Bryan in?"

"He's in the office." He pointed to a corner area.

Bryan Lowe had been born Bryan Lowenstein but had changed his name to Lowe to disguise the fact he was Jewish. He was small, muscular and aggressive, and had had to fight for just about everything all his life. He had started a gym a few years earlier, with the aim of keeping the young lads of the area off the street. He spoke with a nasal tone from having a badly-broken nose that had been hit in and out of the ring. He had a tic, sniffing as he bobbed and weaved like a boxer whilst talking to you. He was a man of many contradictions. Despite hiding his Judaism, he'd fought in the six-day Israeli war in 1967.

Jimmy walked over to a small side room where the door was open. By the sound of it, Bryan was just finishing lecturing a young guy on the error of his ways.

"This is your last chance. Any more fuckin' about and you're out. Got it? So fuckin' get back to training, ok?"

"Yes Bryan," the young lad said obediently, and exited the room.

"See you're still a diplomat, then?"

Bryan looked up. "Stone the crows, Jimmy Watson!" He gave Jimmy a bear hug.

"Listen, they're good kids, but no discipline. Most of their dads fucked off before they were born. What little chance they've got is coming here to work out. Next month, I'm introducing wrestling."

"What – like Jackie Pallo and Mick McManus?"

"Nah, not that play-acting bollocks you see on the telly on a Saturday afternoon. I'm talking about proper grappling. Anyway, how was France?"

"You mean jail."

"Well, yeah."

"Fuckin' great, lovely food and wine."

"Really?"

"No."

Bryan smiled.

"Still a piss taker? What's the coup then?" He bobbed and weaved, throwing a pretend punch into the air.

Jimmy sat down. "I need some help, Bryan. You remember Micky Shit-Tats?"

"Yeah, how could I forget him?"

"Well, things have got a bit out of hand with him. He's already slapped my sister around, and next it could be my old man."

For the next few minutes, Bryan listened to what had happened in Italy and over the last week in London. He leant back, pulling different expressions as the story unfolded. Jimmy finished by saying,

"Basically, I need some muscle to come with me maybe for a meet and give me some protection."

"I'll ask around and see who I can come up with. Anyway, what you up to these days?"

"Working for Lloyd's as an insurance investigator."

"You're fuckin' kidding me?"

"No, I'm a new man. Going back to prison food doesn't appeal to me at all! "

"Fuck me, you goin' straight. What's the world coming to?" He chuckled.

"Changing the subject, your club looks good Bryan, quite an achievement!"

"Well, I'd like to leave a little bit of a legacy, Jimmy."

The two men shook hands. Bryan held on to him and pulled him closer.

"It's good to have you back, my old friend."

*

Jimmy drove back to Primrose Hill, where there was a note waiting for him on the doormat.

"IF YOU WANT TO FIND OUT WHAT HAPPENED TO PETER ENGELS, MEET ME AT UPTON PARK TOMORROW."

Inside the envelope was a ticket for the game the next day. West Ham against Leeds. He was intrigued.

It was match day and at 2.30pm, Jimmy parked about half a mile from the Boleyn ground. He hadn't been to see The Hammers in over ten years. He'd been at Wembley when the West Ham trio of Moore, Hurst and Peters won the World Cup. These days, they were a team that played attractive football, the so-called *West Ham way*, but were now in danger of being relegated, as they'd had a bad run at the start of the season.

He walked up Montpelier Gardens and as he cut through the back streets, Jimmy was surprised to see an old derelict site, dating back to the Second World War, still awaiting development. He remembered playing on it as a kid.

Around Upton Park, a lot of the old East Enders had started to move out to be replaced mainly by Asian families. Every two weeks during the football season, the kids that had roamed these neighbourhoods were now grown men, returning like pilgrims to worship the claret and blue.

He crossed the Barking Road and passed the Cinema showing Caprice, with Richard Harris, the busy pie and mash shop and then bought a small "Happy Hammer" cuddly toy for his sister from the stall on the corner.

He showed his ticket and pushed through the turnstile at the East Stand, still known as the "Chicken Run", named after the wooden structure that used to be there. For away teams, it was especially intimidating as the home fans were so near the pitch. Around ten years earlier, it had been rebuilt, with 3000 seated and 3,500 standing tickets. Jimmy found his seat and sat down. Next to him was empty.

The game was eventful, with the likes of crowd favourites Billy Bonds, Trevor Brooking and "Pop" Robson giving their all on a muddy pitch.

At half time, someone sat next to him. He was wearing a duffel coat with the hood up, but Jimmy could still see enough of the stranger, – it was Peter Engels. Jimmy was shocked to see the man himself. Only a week ago he thought, he'd been murdered, but no, here he was, bold as brass. He leaned into Jimmy. "I hear you've been asking a lot of questions about me," he said, with a Scottish burr. He offered Jimmy a cigarette.

"Back from the dead to watch football?" Asked Jimmy.

Engels held up his collar to protect the lighter flame from the wind and ignored the comment.

"Was always more of a Rangers fan m'self. Used to go to Ibrox with mah old man, it was about the poor bastard's only pleasure. Died in one of those fuckin' horrible tenement blocks aged fifty-eight, where he'd lived all his fuckin' life. You know, when we were wee kids, he used to sleep in a cavity bed; do you know what that is?"

"Sorry I don't," said Jimmy politely.

"It's literally a hole in the fuckin' cavity wall of one of the rooms. That's how fuckin' poor we were. You know, years later, when I came to London, it was like landing on the fuckin' moon. I know what poverty is pal, I 'ain't goin' back to it."

"Faking your own death is a bit desperate, don't yah think?"

"Well, there's a story for sure. Only four years ago I was making a fuckin' fortune, but one thing led to another, including borrowing off the wrong people like Nicky Taylor, and well, here we are and I'm in the shit and to make things worse, I find out you're investigating the case and you've sussed out the poor bastard in the kitchen wasn't me! I got your address and wanted to meet you." Jimmy was puzzled. *How would Engels know that I've guessed he's still alive?*

Jimmy looked straight at Engels.

"You up for turning yourself in?"

"You are fuckin'joking. Even if I wanted to come in and surrender, once that bastard Taylor finds out I'm alive, I'm a dead man. You see, nowhere is safe from him."

"Cure my curiosity, who was it in that kitchen."

"Old mate of mine who was dying. Wanted to leave something for his wife and kids, so we had a little deal that I'd look after them once the insurance is paid out."

It suddenly felt colder; the sodium floodlights fizzed on as the light was starting to fade, and there was a sarcastic cheer from the crowd.

Engels again leant into Jimmy. "What I want is a deal, fifty-fifty, you and me, pal. You tell the insurance company all is well and you have half a million coming your way."

"I'd love to say yes Peter, but I'm sorry, because apart from anything else, I'd get my collar felt."

There was a huge roar as the players came out for the second half. Everybody's eyes turned towards the pitch. Suddenly there was a piercing pain in Jimmy's side. He felt his body temperature shoot up, his vision blurred, and reaching inside his coat, his hand came away covered in blood. He stared at Engels, who stared back, stood up, and calmly walked away.

Jimmy leant forward; it was like a hot poker had been pushed into his body. He fell to his knees and rolled onto the concrete floor. He could hear shouting, but it was like an out-of-body experience, with Jimmy looking down at the events unfolding, and then darkness.

- *Jam Jar- Cockney rhyming slang for car.
- *Monkey -East End slang for £500

CHAPTER SEVEN

Down at the Doctor's

Six hours later, he awoke. As he focussed on the face of a young doctor, Jimmy said, "What happened?"

"West Ham won 2-1."

"Not that, this."

Jimmy raised his head slightly off the pillow; everything hurt like hell.

"Oh, I see," the doctor smiled.

Fuckin' comedian, thought Jimmy.

"Well, I'm Doctor Moss and you're in Whitechapel Hospital and you've been stabbed. Fortunately, the blade didn't penetrate too far, so it missed all vital organs. I'd say your heavy coat and what you had in it probably saved your life."

Jimmy remembered the toy he'd bought for his sister that he'd stuffed in his pocket. *Saved, by a fuckin' teddy bear! You couldn't make it up!*

The doctor continued.

"The wound is about one inch wide and went in about three inches. You're a lucky man!"

"I don't feel lucky, just dizzy."

He felt blood in his hair.

"You hit your head heavily, so I'm sending you down for a CT scan. We'll keep you under observation tonight and if all is ok, we'll discharge you in the morning. Have you any next of kin to contact?"

"Yes, my dad."

"Well, if you give Nurse Simmons here his number, she will contact him and tell him you're ok."

"Please tell him I'm fine and I will be home in the morning. I don't want to panic him."

The nurse smiled. "Of course."

An hour later, he was lying on a different bed with his head in a cradle, rolling into a tunnel-like apparatus.

"Keep perfectly still, best to close your eyes."

The machine buzzed for around ten minutes.

"The scan's all done," said a male nurse.

*

Jimmy didn't get much sleep on the ward that night as next to him was an elderly man who was obviously in a bad mental state and had to be guarded. In the morning the man was gone. Jimmy dozed for a bit and just after eight o'clock, he heard a familiar but unwelcome voice.

"Are you awake, Sleeping Beauty?"

Jimmy opened his eyes slowly.

Standing at the end of the bed were Detective Inspector Wilson and Sergeant Mason. Wilson, an old school classmate, had been trying to arrest Jimmy for years. Mason was a copper he'd known from his dad's local pub.

"You look terrible," said Wilson. Jimmy closed his eyes and mumbled.

"Fuck me, the Ghosts of Christmas Past have come to see me."

"See Mason, our very own clown, and shock horror – I hear he's gone all straight on us!"

"You should try it, Wilson."

Wilson pulled up a chair and sat at the top of the bed near Jimmy. He grabbed some grapes off the neighbouring locker and threw one in the air and caught it in his mouth.

"Now, tell me Poirot, who would want to stab a nice fella like you?"

He spat out a pip across the floor.

"I have no idea," said Jimmy quietly.

"Well, that's funny as a little dickie bird tells me you've upset Nicky Shit-tats and he's back in London looking to teach you a lesson. I don't know what you did, but apparently, he's spitting feathers. What you really up to son?"

"Not much, just a bit of work for Lloyd's," he said, matter-of-factly.

"Ooh, do you hear that Mason, our Watson's an INVESTIGATOR just like his namesake. Who would fuckin' believe it? Elementary my dear Watson," he said in a terrible posh voice. Mason laughed on cue.

He spat out another pip. Jimmy said nothing. Jimmy said nothing, he closed his eyes, wishing them to go away.

Wilson insisted on giving Jimmy a history lesson.

"Well Mason, let me tell you about our mate, Shit-Tats and his old man George Taylor, who made his money scamming gullible punters. He'd tell a face, that he was making a fortune on a little tip he'd been given through a good friend. He'd give them the outline of the non-existent investment, be it oil from Texas or gold from Australia or any old bollocks, and then go quiet on them. Being greedy, they are now desperate to be in on the deal and of course George duly obliges.

Now he would keep the punter dangling for months, sometimes for years, and right at the moment the punter thinks he's getting his money, he would announce a tragedy and sadly, all the money's gone. All told with great sincerity of course.

Unfortunately, one day George picks on the wrong punter and disappears in a puff of smoke. Rumour has it that he is currently propping up a flyover in Stratford. And guess what? That wrong punter was none other than Frankie Fontana. No doubt this sped Micky's departure out of the country, along with a few other reasons. I guess Micky had to forgive his father-in-law, or he would have joined poor old George in the road works. So, my son, these are the nice sort of people you're messing with."

Mason pulled a face of surprise and nodded.

Wilson stood up and ran his fingers through his greasy hair. Looking out of the window, he said,

"Are you gonna tell us anything Watson?"

"Would like to, but it's all blank," said Jimmy innocently.

Wilson turned back just as a nurse appeared at the foot of the bed.

"C'mon Mason, we're wasting our time here! I've warned you Jimmy."

They both abruptly left.

"You having breakfast Jimmy?" The nurse smiled as if she knew him.

"Why not?"

Just after nine o'clock, Dr Moss was doing his rounds. After looking at Jimmy's notes, he said, "You're doing well, so we'll be able to discharge you this morning, but get plenty of rest. You'll be sore for a bit, so I've prescribed you some painkillers that you can collect from the pharmacy. We'll have you back in a couple of weeks to have your stitches out, but take it easy."

"Thank you, Doctor."

At that moment, Jimmy's dad arrived in the ward and made his way to his bed. He crouched down and touched Jimmy's cheek the way he used to when he was a little boy.

"Hello Son, how yah doin'?"

He could see his dad's eyes filling up.

"Been better dad."

"I'm worried son how this is all going to end."

"It'll be all right, you ok to take me home?"

Within an hour they were outside the entrance of Whitechapel Hospital, and they hailed a cab. Jimmy struggled up the stairs to his flat, feeling tired and as uncomfortable as hell. As they got to the front door, they could see it had been kicked in. Inside, everything had been either smashed or cut up. Jimmy stood in the middle of his lounge, looking around in disbelief.

The flat was uninhabitable. Even his clothes were ripped to bits. Even that bloody carriage clock had finally got smashed!

"Fuck me," he exclaimed as he surveyed the damage.

"Come home with me son, you need to rest up."

Another taxi took them to his dad's, where Jimmy told him about the stabbing.

"For fuck's sake Jimmy," his dad exclaimed, taking in all Jimmy had just told him.

"All right if I use the phone?"

"Of course." Jimmy dialled Lowe's number.

"Bryan, it's Jimmy. Any news?"

"I've got a contact on Canvey called Sly, who can send three of his boys. They wanna meet us tonight at the Connaught Tavern in Silvertown around 11pm."

"That's fine."

That afternoon, Jimmy fell asleep on his dad's sofa. At 9pm his sister woke him up.

"Jimmy, you ok? Dad's done you some dinner."

Jimmy carefully put his feet down on the carpet. His sister looked at him with exasperation.

"Dad's told me about what happened at West Ham. Jimmy, you should get out of London."

"I can't."

He grimaced and held his side as he staggered to his feet.

Alison looked at him.

"Never a fuckin' dull moment with you, is there?"

Jimmy couldn't eat and announced to his dad he was going out.

"You're fuckin' mad son!"

As he left, his dad called after him.

"Be careful Jimmy." It seemed that danger was drawing the two of them closer.

*

At 11pm that night, Jimmy and Bryan were sitting in his Cortina in the deserted car park of the Connaught Tavern by the Albert Dock. Already nature had started to take over the deserted docks, with grass, wildflowers and silver birch trees sprouting through the tarmac.

Bryan shuffled in his seat, snorted and twitched. He checked his watch.

"What are we expecting, Bryan?"

"I'm hoping for some hard geezers with shooters, looking the part, ready to frighten the shit out of anyone."

Another ten minutes passed, when headlights appeared on the road and a car swung into the car park. Jimmy could see three big lumps squeezed into a Ford Fiesta. The driver was so big, he looked like he was wearing the car rather than just steering it. They pulled up next to the Cortina.

Bryan nodded and they got out and slid into the back of the 1600E, the three of them still in dinner suits.

"Looking smart boys. You didn't have to dress up for us." Said Bryan smiling. They didn't get the joke.

One of them said,

We've just left the doors at TOTS to come 'ere."

With the best part of half a ton of bouncers in the back, the rear suspension creaked, and the front wings rose. Jimmy felt a bit like Fred Flintstone.

"For a moment I thought you three were a Rat Pack tribute act!"

"What's a Rat Pack?" one of them said in a dozey voice.

"Never mind," said Jimmy. He turned and shook their hands. There were no smiles or laughs.

"I'm Reg."

"I'm Gary."

"I'm Shane," said the happy threesome.

Bryan spoke.

"We've got a bit of bovva and I've been told you boys are Sly's best men to sort it out."

Bryan had a quick twitch.

"What's the problem then?" said Reg.

"Micky Shit-Tats is the problem!"

Reg looked at Shane, Shane looked at Gary.

"Fuck me, I'm not getting involved with that mad "fucker," said Reg.

"Nor me."

"Or me."

There was silence, followed by the sound of the Three Wise Men of Canvey sliding out of the car. They bundled back into the little Fiesta as fast as possible and drove away like their lives depended on it.

"Well Bryan, that went well, they couldn't get away quick enough. It was as if a fuckin' fire alarm went off!"

"Sorry Jimmy, I fawt they'd be ok. What d'you wanna do now?"

"Fucked if I know."

After dropping Bryan home, Jimmy remembered an old contact of his that might still be in the security business. He'd ring him when he got home.

CHAPTER EIGHT

Message in a Bottle

"Good evening, Hawk Security," came the voice in a heavy South African accent. Jimmy knew it well. It was his least favourite accent, along with Brummy. It had always struck Jimmy that South Africans sort of talk with their mouths almost totally shut, like ventriloquists.

Greg Radford had been travelling across Europe in the sixties, escaping the chaos in Rhodesia where he'd served in the military. In London he'd met an Irishman called Mick O'Hara and gone to work the doors as a bouncer for him. Mick was as hard as nails, ex-just about everything, he'd no doubt done some naughty things back home. Over the years, Radford had become his right-hand man and was now running O'Hara's business for him, who'd retired to Ireland.

"Greg, it's Jimmy Watson."

"How's things my friend? It's been a long time, Buddy!"

"I've had some trouble from a guy named Nicky Taylor."

Greg chuckled. "I know that bastard. We've had a few run-ins with him and his boys over the years. Fucked off to Italy, didn't he?"

"He did, but he's back and he seems to have me in his sights."

Jimmy summarised the previous week's events.

"Jimmy, can you meet me at ten tomorrow at Greasy Bill's caff near the flyover in Barking?"

"Yeah sure, I know where it is."

"I'll do a bit of digging around in the meantime."

*

The next morning at Greasy Bills Radford and O'Hara sat down opposite Jimmy. They were both big, tall men, but quiet and polite. Still, you wouldn't want to get on their wrong side. Greasy Bill clumsily placed the breakfasts in front of them. Jimmy was surprised to see O'Hara.

"Three Heart Attacks on a Plate. Any sauces?" Said Greasy.

"All good," said O'Hara.

Radford opened the conversation.

"Mick's just flown in from Shannon, Jimmy."

"Oh really, how come?"

O'Hara stuck a fork into one of his sausages and talked while waving it around in his hand.

"Greg runs the show over here now, but when I heard the problem was our mutual friend, I was on the first plane out. One of my guys laid Shit-Tats out on his back in a club in Romford, and then he took a serious beating by some of Shit-Tats' boys. As of today, we're on to that bastard. We've already petrol-bombed two of his father-in-law's trucks early this morning. I think he's got the message."

Jimmy felt a shudder of fear run through him.

"Christ Mick," I thought Greg was gonna check him out and maybe arrange a meet, not start some fuckin' sixties turf war; I need to calm things down, not wind them up."

"Jimmy, you don't get to calm down those arseholes, you have to fight fire with fire," said O'Hara.

Jimmy sat back exasperated. The exact opposite of what he wanted was happening.

Greg Radford continued, "You don't ever appease those fuckers. You know, we can give you twenty-four-hour security."

"I don't want fuckin' twenty-four-hour security; I want a fuckin' big problem sorted."

O'Hara looked at Greg and smiled. "Well, let's see what response we get."

"I think I can guess the response, boys, and I appreciate your help, but please don't do anything just now. I will call you in the next few days."

"We're here to help," said O'Hara winking. He knew their intentions were good, but now they were a liability.

Jimmy finished his breakfast, picked up his keys and paid. He knew he had to push these boys away from the situation, as they were just making matters worse.

He left the caff and drove straight to Barking, parking up in Ripple Road. He walked up the hill opposite the station and into the courtyard where Chains nightclub was located. It was run by Charlie Brooks, one of his friends from school, who used to live down the street. He was known as "Champagne Charlie", as he loved *all things bright and beautiful!* Decked out in designer wear, with his Rolex and spikey Rod Stewart haircut, he was certainly noticed when he walked into a room.

Over a ten-year period, he had created an upmarket club for the over-twenty-fives of Essex. His boast was: *You could meet a better class of bird at Chains*!

Jimmy squeezed past a red Ferrari Dino parked in front of the main doors and walked into the foyer where a young guy was hoovering. Jimmy raised his voice:

"Is Champagne around?"

The guy turned off the Hoover.

"Who's asking?"

"I'm an old friend."

"He's in his office doing some staff training." He nodded towards an area in a corner.

Jimmy approached a blue door in a dimly-lit corridor. He heard the hoover switch back on. As the door opened, he was taken aback by the sight of a big white arse going back and forth on top of what looked like quite an attractive woman. Jimmy quickly shut the door and walked back into the club. The young guy smiled.

"Still training the staff, is he?"

"Very funny."

"Tell Champagne, Jimmy Watson called in, and I will wait in Percy Ingles' for him."

"Yeah, I'll tell him," said the smiling kid.

"Wanker," mumbled Jimmy.

Twenty minutes later, Champagne entered Percy's, and as he walked towards where Jimmy was sitting, he said to the lady behind the counter, "Milky coffee love, and two egg rolls please."

His hair was dyed blonde, long and spikey and gelled upwards. It gave him the look of having just arrived on a motorbike.

He was wearing a Sergio Tacchini tracksuit, with a cigarette burning away in his hand.

"Oi oi Saveloy! Long time, no see! Sorry about the... well you know, catching me 'aving a bit of horizontal refreshment!"

"You still married to Carol?"

"Naughty! In fact, divorced after ten years together, then there was a second Mrs Brooks, called Sharon, that only lasted two years. As much as I like wedding cake, I don't fink there'll be a third wife, especially as I'm now forty-one, footloose and fancy free. It's difficult in this game, Jimmy, you know 'ow it is, odd hours, odd birds around you all the time and after all, I'm only human! Anyway, to what do I owe the pleasure?"

"Micky Shit-Tats worked for you, didn't he? Are you still mates?"

"We were never mates as such, but yeah, we got on alright, a bit of a thick bastard though. Obviously marrying into the Fontana's gave 'im some clout, but he turned into a fuckin' nuisance to them, what with dealing drugs to kids and winding people up that he shouldn't. He got involved in a stabbing in Mooro's in Stratford. That's why they shoved him off to Italy, along with the trouble with his old man. I haven't heard from him since. Why'd you ask?"

Jimmy explained what had been happening.

"Fuck me Jimmy, of all the people to upset, you do not want it to be Frankie fuckin' Fontana! You don't wanna' start a fight you can't win. Let me get you a meet to see if we can get things sorted."

The egg rolls arrived with a coffee. The woman serving him was around thirty years of age. As she leant over, Champagne said, "Nice pair!"

"Cheeky bleeder!"

"Of eggs love!"

"Funny, arncha!"

"She loves me really," Champagne laughed, picking up one of his rolls.

She walked back to the counter, smiling.

*

"Cor, she's a bit of all right. Could be my next bit of staff training," he joked.

Ten minutes later, both men were back at the club. Champagne got a phone book out of his desk drawer.

"Let me try this number."

He dialled it.

"Morning, Is that Frankie? It's Charlie Brooks... yeah that's right, Champagne. I'm with a good friend of mine, Jimmy Watson, who seems to have had a misunderstanding with Nicky, and would like to resolve things. Can we meet with you both? I know Nicky well, you might remember, he used to work for me."

Jimmy watched Champagne as he pulled faces listening to the reply, nodding continuously.

"Yes, I understand, we will be there at four today."

He put down the phone.

"Well?" said Jimmy.

"The old man Frankie is fuckin' raging. He said two of his skip lorries got torched last night, so he's more than keen to meet you! What were you thinking of?"

"Look, I only asked someone I know to check him out, and it all went tits up!"

"Now there's an understatement. You got your meeting Jimmy, but we've got to be careful."

CHAPTER NINE

With a Little Luck

Four hours later, the two of them pulled up in King Street by the abandoned Covent Garden Market. He hadn't known the market had moved to Battersea in 1974, as at that time he was still in prison.

A grey hoarding surrounded the whole area he'd known as a kid, and it was sad to see how derelict it had all become. Even the underground station was now closed at weekends because the area was like a ghost town. As a thirteen-year-old, he would come here with an old school friend, Davey Long, whose dad had had a flower business. The market was split between fruit & veg and flower businesses. In those days, lorries would be driven through the night from all over the country, delivering all sorts, oranges from Spain to vegetables from Norfolk. Generations had worked there all their lives. The work shifts would begin around midnight when the deliveries started coming in. Goods would be loaded by hand with old-fashioned barrows and upright trollies charging along the aisles. Jimmy could remember being taken to Albert's or Frank's for a mug of tea and a sausage sandwich. The place would be in full swing by 6am with the rush over by 10.30am, at which point, the old flower ladies would wander around looking for a deal.

Now that way of life was gone, all in the name of progress.

Champagne did his coat up and said, "Jimmy, when we get in there, let me do the talking. Shit-Tats knows me and trusts me, so don't try to justify anything. The most I want you to do is nod or grunt. We've got one chance to get you out of this mess, so just say nuffink."

They walked along Bedford Street to a set of gates in the hoarding that had been left unlocked for them. As they entered, Jimmy immediately recognised the main concourse, no longer full of buyers and sellers but littered with rubbish and broken barrows and shelves. Some of the glass skylights were broken and hundreds of pigeons were now nesting in the vaulted ceilings. The floor was splattered with bird waste and feathers.

Jimmy and Champagne made their way through the columned passageways. The iron and stone pillars stretched upwards, forgotten monuments of a glorious, discarded past. It was a stunning building and its beauty still shone through the darkness and dirt.

The big glass lanterns he remembered so well were still intact. *Surely, they won't demolish this place*, he thought. *But what do you do with such a relic in the middle of London?*

"'Ello!" Champagne shouted along a dark corridor, where they could see a light in the distance. A slight, ugly man came towards them on the central concourse. The sound of his footsteps echoed loudly.

"Come on, follow me," he said impatiently. He had a heavy Mancunian accent. He stopped and turned, shaking his head disapprovingly.

"You fuckers don't know what you've started. Arms out," he demanded and patted them down.

He led Jimmy and Charlie into a large, darkly lit room. It was the former office for management of the City of London staff at Covent Garden. 1940s signs adorned the room. The place smelt of dampness, with moss-covered skylights struggling to let the daylight through. Jimmy shivered slightly. Cold or fear? He wasn't sure. Micky Shit-Tats was sitting at an old boardroom table, next to someone who he presumed was his father-in-law, Frankie Fontana, sitting with his hands resting out on the table in front of him. On the two outside fingers of each hand were chunky gold rings that no doubt had smashed into many a face. He wore a long camel-coloured coat and Micky had a long black leather one that matched his wig. Jimmy thought he looked like a bad Johnny Cash, but there'd be no singing tonight, not the musical variety, anyway! Leaning against a wall, was the Bullet-Head from Rome, (who obviously hadn't perished).

Champagne went over to Shit-Tats and man-hugged him affectionately and went into full charm mode.

"Looking good, son!"

"Yeah Charlie, I was, until this prick came along." He looked at Jimmy.

Jimmy looked at Fontana; he'd heard of him but never met him. He was in his late sixties with the usual combed-back grey hairstyle all these old East End gangsters seemed to have. You could tell in his younger days he would have been quite a handsome man. However, as he turned his head, a large scar could be seen, running from the side of his mouth down to the top of his neck.

"Sit down boys," Fontana said quietly.

The two of them sat down, with Manchester Man leaning up against a wall with his arms folded. Leaning in a corner against another wall, was Bullet Head. Fontana leant forward stared at Champagne, and in a gravelly aggressive voice said, "Tell me son, why should we let your friend walk out of here after burning two of me fuckin' motors?"

"Well, that wasn't Jimmy."

"Fuckin' coincidence then!" Shouted Shit-Tats.

"Exactly."

We I don't believe in coincidences," said Fontana calmly.

Shit-Tats leaned forward.

"That fuckin' South African Greg whatever his fuckin' name is, was seen leaving Frankie's yard. I fuckin' know he's a mate of yours Jimmy, so don't even think about telling me you had nothing to do with it."

Jimmy looked at Shit-Tats and then looked at Fontana.

"I asked Greg to help out, but I had no idea he'd do what he did."

Champagne glared at Jimmy as if to warn, *Don't say another word.*

Shit-Tats theatrically banged the table with his right fist.

"Two of Frankie's motors, plus back in Italy I've got a smashed-up Maserati and one of my guys in hospital wrapped up like as fuckin' mummy. You paying for those, son?" Bullet Head was nodding in agreement.

"How much we talking?" said Champagne.

"Fifteen grand."

"And two grand for the inconvenience," the little northern guy chipped in.

"You fuckin' kidding me?" said Jimmy.

"Another grand for swearing."

"Fuck off!"

"That's another grand."

Champagne cut in.

"Gentlemen please. If fifteen grand will resolve this, this misunderstanding well, fifteen grand it is."

Jimmy struggled to keep quiet. *Where was he going to get fifteen grand from*?

Frankie looked at Champagne and then flashed a look at Jimmy.

"Ok, you get us the money, but I don't want to see fuck-face or hear from him again. You got me?" He looked again at Jimmy. "Count yourself as lucky, and if you see that big fuckin' African, tell him we will be paying him a visit."

Yet again, Jimmy was being told how lucky he was!

"You happy Nicky son?" said Fontana, looking at Shit-Tats.

"No, but, It'll do for now."

There was a silence, then Champagne spoke.

"Can you give me a few days? That's a lot of dough to pull up."

"Ten grand tomorrow and another five in seven days," said Fontana.

"Ok, I'll do my best." Fontana leaned back and said, "Yeah, you better."

The room went deathly quiet. Champagne stood up.

"Well thank you, gentlemen. Come on Jim."

Jimmy stood up obediently. *Is that it?* He thought to himself.

As they left, Shit-Tat's voice followed them. "'Ow's that sister of yours?"

Jimmy saw Bullet Head smile but didn't reply. *Bastard*, he thought.

"Hope you like the way we rearranged your flat for you," said Bullet Head.

Still, Jimmy didn't react.

They walked back along the concourse; they could hear laughter coming from the room they'd just left.

"Charlie," Jimmy said quietly, "I haven't got a spare fifteen quid never mind fifteen grand."

"Jimmy, I don't think you appreciate: with a little luck, we've just bought your life back for you. Even if you have to sell everything, just do it. They are fucking animals. They live by a completely different set of rules to us. Tell your friend at Lloyd's you're out of it, these guys don't mess about. Most people don't come out of that room. If they do, they're usually horizontal."

Jimmy thought for a few moments.

"Sorry, you're right, I appreciate you sticking your neck out for me."

*

Jimmy dropped Charlie back to Barking and drove on to his father's place.

"Well, how'd it go?" Said his dad anxiously.

"As well as could be expected. How's Alison?"

"She's better. She's out with this new fella. Cuppa tea?"

"Why not?"

The two of them sat up watching TV, waiting for Alison to get in, just like an old married couple.

Just after midnight she opened the front door.

"And what time do you call this?" Jimmy joked.

His sister smiled. "Everything ok?"

"All sorted, sorry about the roughing up you got at my place."

Don't worry, it's all forgotten Jim."

"Well, what's the name of your new man?"

"Philip Cohen."

"Married?"

"Sort of!"

"Look, as long as he makes you happy, who cares?"

"How's your side?" she asked.

"Sore."

"Take it easy Jimmy." She gave him a peck on the cheek. "I've got an early start in the morning."

"I bet you have."

She smiled, and it reminded him of when they were both a lot younger. His dad shook his head disapprovingly of what he'd just heard and went to bed and Jimmy curled up on the settee.

*

At six the next morning, there was a loud banging on the door. Jimmy peered out from behind a curtain, and standing at the front doorstep looking up were Wilson and Mason.

Fuckin' hell. What do those two want? He thought.

Jimmy put on his trousers and shirt and opened the door.

"Morning boys, fuckin' lonely, are we?"

Wilson held his hand up and turned his back as he coughed a smoker's cough loudly.

"Reckon it's time you gave up the fags, Wilson," said Jimmy.

"Reckon for once you might be of use to us, Sherlock. Get your shoes on will yah, and come with us."

"What for?"

"We've got a nice man hanging upside down in a warehouse for you to say hello to. You comin'?"

"How could I refuse?"

Jimmy put on some socks and shoes and got into the back of an unmarked Ford Granada. The high-speed drive to the Highway in Wapping, took around fifteen minutes. The car pulled up in Glasshouse Fields, a narrow, cobbled street, where at the end was an old red-brick factory building with a large yard area to the front. An ancient sign was leaning dangerously forward above the entrance door, that read "The Chelvedon Knitting Company." Parked outside was a Police Rover.

Wilson turned to Jimmy. "Come see!"

The three men got out. It was a cold morning, made even colder by the fact that Jimmy was only in a shirt. He followed Wilson and Mason into the factory. As he entered, all he could see were huge old Victorian knitting machines, cobwebs instead of thread hanging across them. Jimmy could see that some had the date 1900 stamped on them.

"Look at this place," said Wilson. "Same old story, old family firms ripping the money out for years. No wonder we can't compete."

"You wanna soap box," joked Jimmy.

They made their way between machines and discarded stools and tables. As they entered another part of the factory floor through a metal door, Jimmy recognised the body that was hanging from a steel beam by a chain wrapped around his feet. It was an upside-down Peter Engels. His shirt hung open, revealing a badly beaten face and body. His arms were outstretched, with blood still running off his fingertips. A police pathologist had just arrived at the scene.

"This your mate, Peter Engels?"

"Yeah, it's him alright."

"Whoever did this liked his work," said Mason. "He's had a hammering, quite literally. His interrogator would have been covered in blood. Almost everything has been struck with a hammer. You can see the round marks all over him."

Engels rotated slightly in the draft blowing through the factory.

Wilson lit a cigarette.

"Well, Sherlock fuckin' Holmes, what sort of bastard do you know that would do this?"

Jimmy stood there, hands in pockets, staring at the hanging corpse.

Wilson continued.

"Well, someone wanted the body found. Usually, with a gangland killing, they sling the body into the Thames to be sucked under the false dock, never to be seen again. No, the bastards that did this wanted him found alright."

"I'd be knocking on Micky Shit-Tats' door if I were you. He's waiting for a payout through Engels," said Jimmy.

Wilson stubbed out his cigarette and looked at Jimmy.

"Well, he's in no state to pay fuck-all now! What a way to end up."

"I think you'll find he's worth more dead than living," said Jimmy.

"Mason, get one of the uniforms to drop Columbo here home and we'll pay a visit to Shit-Tats."

*

After twenty-four hours of hearing nothing, Jimmy rang Wilson at Marylebone Police Station.

"Wilson, it's Jimmy Watson. Any joy with Shit-Tats?"

"Visited him at his flat, clean as a whistle, nice tight alibi. We can't touch him, not yet anyway, unless someone grasses on him. We've got some ears out, so we'll see." With that, the line went dead.

Jimmy knew Wilson was a bent copper, so for all he knew, he may have been paid off. There was no point waiting for the Wilsons of this world, so Jimmy decided it was time to make a move on Shit-Tats himself. He dialled the number of an old friend.

"Bob, it's Jimmy, I've got a job for you."

CHAPTER TEN

Burn Baby Burn

At 7.20 the next morning, Handbag Bob sat in the driver's seat of his green Triumph Dolomite in Montague Square, Paddington. The Square was famous ten years earlier for being the former home of Beatle John Lennon and before that, Jimi Hendrix. Handbag had been watching the front of Number 15 all night.

Suddenly, the door of the Triumph opened, and Jimmy got in with two takeaway teas and some toast.

"How's it going Bob?"

"You mean, apart from freezing me bollocks off?"

"Don't worry, you'll soon be back in the arms of that Brazilian bird you were telling me about!"

"Jimmy, she's bloody exhausting: legs like the M1, they go on and on! She's like a contortionist. At least being here last night gave me a rest! Apart from the sex, she wants to go out all the time. Thing is, all her mates are twenty years younger than me, so I feel a bit, well... old."

"You need to get someone your own age, so you can stay in and watch telly."

"Tell me about it. What about you Jim, how are you doin'?"

"Apart from being stabbed and bloody sore, absolutely fine."

"No woman in your life then?"

"I don't seem to be very good at that sort of thing. This is for you." Jimmy handed him the takeaway. "Anything happen?" Jimmy looked across the square.

"Got here at nine last night. Old Shit-Tats came back with a bird around midnight and she left around seven. Got a decent polaroid this morning as she left."

Jimmy looked at the picture.

"Blimey." The look of surprise prompted Hand Bag to ask, "You know her?"

"It's Engels' wife, or should I say, second wife who's not actually his wife. She's still plain old Karen Watkins, as he never divorced his first Missus."

Handbag chuckled. "So, she's knobbing Shit-Tats! What a joke. Hadn't seen him in years! What's with the wig?"

"Search me!"

"Do you reckon he wears it in bed?" Laughed Handbag,

"Fuck knows!" Shrugged Jimmy.

"Looks a right wanker!"

Jimmy looked at Handbag and said, "The irony is, they both think she's about to get a big insurance payout but she's gonna get fuck-all. I'd like to be a fly on that wall when the news comes through." Handbag tapped Jimmy's arm.

"Looky-looky, heads up, looks like you're just in time to see your mate leave."

Jimmy looked across the street. Shit-Tats was dressed as usual in black. He stood on the steps outside his flat and lit a cigarette, then got into a blue Bentley S with a 1964 number plate.

"Obviously keeping a low profile," Jimmy laughed. The Bentley roared out of the square.

Handbag sipped some more coffee and said, "Show-time son. There's no alarm, I've checked. If he comes back, I'll hit the car horn."

Jimmy walked across the road and pushed a skeleton key into an old Yale lock, but it failed to turn. However, the second key he used turned the lock. He entered a black-and-white-tiled hallway that led to a large drawing room. In the middle of the floor parallel to a tall marble fireplace were two huge maroon settees with a stool between them. Above the fireplace was a round ornate mirror with wall lights either side. Around the room were various chairs and small tables with a roll-top desk against one of the walls. The bookcase had a collection of books so tatty they would shame a boot sale. The wooden floor was covered by three different rugs, one of which had a stuffed eagle mounted on a plinth sitting on top of it. The décor could easily have been called Anglo-Scottish junk. This Jimmy suspected was a room put together by an interior designer, who would've used words like richness and elegance, but was anything but.

On a small table was a Bakelite phone, next to which was a notebook. Jimmy flicked over the first page; it read: *Karen*. On the next page was another note*: Tell him to wait for you at your place today at 5pm.*

Was this the instruction that had lured Peter Engels to his death?

He entered the bedroom. Like the rest of the apartment, it was a mess. There was a big unmade bed dominating it. On the dressing table was a wig on a stand, giving out a somewhat spooky vibe. By the bedside on a glass-topped locker was a discarded razor blade, lying on a film of coke powder next to an open packet of cigarettes. Jimmy opened the wardrobe; all the clothes were black. The drawers had a selection of underwear and jumpers also in black.

Back in the drawing room, Jimmy walked over to the roll-top desk, but there was nothing in it. The kitchen had an empty Champagne bottle on the work surface and two empty glasses. One had lipstick smeared along the edge. There wasn't much else to see.

Jimmy made his way to the front door and left the building and crossed the square to Handbag's car.

"Blimey, that was quick, any clues?"

"Maybe, there was a note that might mean something."

"What now?"

"Drop us off at the Lloyd's offices could yah?"

*

Twenty minutes later, Jimmy made his way up to Ward's office.

With a smile Amanda said, "Ah, morning early bird. Shall I see if Lesley's free?"

"Please."

She tapped on Ward's door.

"Go in Jimmy."

She stood back for him to pass. He sat down in front of Lesley Ward and shared his thoughts on what had happened over the last few days. Her fingertips pressed against her temples. She looked up.

"Jimmy, you won't like this, but we've decided to pay out the claim to Engels' wife, his only wife come to that!"

"You gotta be kidding me?"

"I'm afraid the powers that be have spoken."

"Lesley, it's obvious there's one massive scam going on here."

"Sorry Jimmy, there's a lot of maybe-this and maybe-that, but it doesn't alter the fact that Peter Engels is dead and he was insured. You did well. There'll be a nice cheque in the post and hopefully we will do some more work together."

She went silent and it was obvious she was waiting for him to leave. He got up. The sudden termination of the investigation deflated him. The carpet had well and truly been pulled from underneath him. There'd be no celebration of catching the deceivers he felt were in his grasp.

Lesley continued looking down at the papers on her desk.

"See you around Lesley."

"I hope so," she said without looking up.

*

Jimmy took the lift down feeling puzzled. *How could Lesley give in so easily?*

He couldn't resist it: he just needed to get the truth out of Karen Engels. Half an hour later, he parked in Beak Street, it was busy with tourists. He got to the café but could see no one. Chairs were stacked on the tables. He pushed the door, it was unlocked.

"Karen, are you in?"

There was no reply. He could hear a noise coming from upstairs. He got to the top just in time to see Shit-Tats deliver a ferocious punch to Karen Engels' face. The force which knocked her back, rocked her head against a glass cabinet, smashing the glass and the ornaments inside it. Her blood seemed to be everywhere. She'd already taken a hell of a beating. As she slumped to the floor, Shit-Tats turned to face Jimmy and growled.

"You're like a fuckin' bad penny."

He ran at Jimmy and caught him with a blow to the jaw, knocking him over a small couch. Jimmy lay on his back, dazed. His stab wound ached. He was in no shape for any sort of fight. Shit-Tats reached down and grabbed him by his shirt. As Jimmy desperately tried to get away, Shit-tats hit him again. He scrambled to his feet and made a run for the open door, but the two men collided, both tumbling down the stairs, into the café kitchen. Jimmy got up first and grabbed a carving knife, pointing it at Shit-Tats.

"Like the old days Jimmy, eh?"

Shit-Tats moved from side to side. He actually seemed to be enjoying the confrontation. He continued.

"Think you'd get away with taking the piss out of me, did yah son?"

Jimmy slashed at him, but Shit-Tats was laughing like a madman.

"C'mon son, you can do betta than that," he grinned.

Jimmy had to think fast. He grabbed a pan still simmering, full of cooking oil, and threw it at Shit-Tats who saw it coming and turned away, shielding his face with his left hand. The fat burnt his hand and had caught his sleeve and the back of his coat and wig.

"You fucker," he said, flexing his blistering hand.

Suddenly, behind Shit-Tats, a battered Karen Engels appeared. She picked up an oven-lighter gun and flicked it on and shoved it into his oil-covered wig. A huge flame engulfed his head as the oil over his body ignited. He span and screamed, ripping his wig off, but it was too late. The fire had leapt to his back and arms. He crashed to the floor, rolling, and continuing to scream. They could have helped him, but instead they both stood and stared. Jimmy and Karen watched with a mixture of horror and relief as he rolled about on the floor, screaming, until there was just silence. Smoke and the sickening smell of burnt flesh filled the room.

There was a certain irony that he should die this way.

Karen Engels sat on the bottom step of the stairs and wept. Jimmy picked up the phone and called 999.

*

An hour later DI Wilson was standing over the charred body.

"Another fucking dead crook! They're falling like fuckin' flies around you mate. I'll be able to retire at this rate. What's your secret?"

Jimmy stared at the body and put a comforting arm around Karen Engels.

"It's over, you're safe now."

Wilson looked down at them.

"Ah, how sweet," he sneered.

"Don't forget, I need a statement from you two."

CHAPTER ELEVEN

Holiday in The Sun

May arrived, and Jimmy decided to call into Karen Engels' café to see how she was doing. He never did get that confession of her involvement he was hoping for. Another pressing matter was what would Palermo Frankie do, now that his son-in-law had been killed? It had been over a month since his death.

Through the glass front of the café, he could see Karen's sister; he tapped on the window. She opened the door.

"It's Jimmy, isn't it?"

"Yes, that's right, how's Karen?"

"She's good. Thank God it's all over."

"Is she around?"

"No, she's taking a well-earned holiday."

"Oh, good for her. How long is she away for?"

"Just a week, she went yesterday."

"Where'd she go to?"

"What's that island where Gracie Fields lives?"

Jimmy thought for a moment.

"Oh, Capri."

"That's it!" She smiled.

"Alright for some! When are you reopening?"

"We aren't. Me and me sister are selling up and moving on to pastures new."

"Well, good luck with whatever you do."

She smiled, "Thanks," and locked the door as Jimmy left.

*

The following morning, Jimmy was sitting in his kitchen, unshaven, feeling anxious. He felt he needed direction, and he certainly didn't want to slide back to where he was before the Engels job.

The letter box flapped. He walked over and bent down and picked up an envelope. Inside was a cheque from Lloyd's for £10,000. *Fuckin' hell, maybe I will stick with this game after all*, he thought. He excitedly picked up the phone and dialled Ward's office.

"Giles Burgess' office." It was Amanda's voice.

"Amanda, could I speak to Lesley to thank her for payment… and who's Giles Burgess anyway?"

"I thought she would have told you," she replied. "Lesley resigned, deciding to take early retirement. Giles is her replacement. Said it had all got a bit too much for her. Have to admit, we were all shocked. We'd thought the only way she would leave Lloyd's was in a box! Still, she's probably sunning herself in Capri as we speak."

Suddenly, alarm bells rang. Both Ward and Karen Engels in Capri at the same time?

"I don't suppose you have a number abroad for her, Amanda?"

"Afraid not."

"Ok, would you mind giving me her home address, so I can send her flowers when she's back?"

There were a few seconds of silence. Jimmy guessed Amanda was trying to process whether or not she should give him the address.

"As it's you," she said, and read it to him.

*

Two hours later, he was turning the key into Lesley Ward's flat in St John's Wood. It was typical of the type of block built in the 1930s, when the ground floor in those days would have had a social club where residents would meet, sadly though, these disappeared by the end of the war. Inside, there were two bedrooms and a lounge both decorated art deco style. What was unusual were, there were no pictures on the wall.

Jimmy started his search by going through the papers on the desk, but apart from a few bills, there was nothing of interest. As he walked into the kitchen, on the worktop he could see a Collins desktop diary. He leafed through it. On the page for May 8th was the address and phone number of a restaurant with 1pm written next to it. From Ward's lounge Jimmy called the number and a man's voice said,

"Sunset Restaurant Capri." Jimmy hung up.

What the fuck was going on? Engels and Ward being in Capri at the same time. This was no coincidence.

There was only one way to get to the bottom of this, he'd go out to the Sunset Restaurant in Italy himself to see who would turn up at 1pm tomorrow.

*

That night at 6pm, Jimmy boarded a plane to Naples. On landing, a forty-minute taxi ride took him to the boat terminal. Although it was getting late, it was still warm as he hung over the rails of the ferry. He stepped onto Capri at just gone 10pm, where he caught a cab to Anacapri. At an elderly receptionist handed him a key.

"Enjoy your stay signor. "Any plans?"

"Just taking a little holiday in the sun," Jimmy smiled.

The following morning, Jimmy woke up and took a swig of water from his bedside table. He walked over to the window. The view over the bay in Anacapri was beautiful, it was a shame he had no one to share it with. He showered and dressed and made his way to breakfast. The hotel had only fourteen rooms and was more a romantic retreat rather than a place for a single man. He sat on the terrace drinking tea and eating a continental breakfast, while thinking about the previous few weeks' events.

When he'd finished, he went to the lobby to order a cab for later that morning, but the driver from the hotel insisted on dropping Jimmy to his destination, which he gratefully accepted. At 12.30pm as the hotel's old Fiat taxi descended a steep road, a white MGC sports car pulled out in front of them and accelerated away. The car was a real rarity in these parts. In the driver's seat was the distinct figure of Lesley Ward. The driver smiled, "Pretty lady."

The straight six engine of the MG roared in front of them with Ward pushing through the gears. He nearly said, "Follow that car," but instead said "Keep close behind her."

Both cars passed the oncoming buses and taxis with little room for error, making no attempt to slow down. The Fiat stayed around a hundred yards behind, all the way down to the bay. Jimmy found himself gripping the seat. *What is it with these Italians and their driving?*

The driver shouted above the sound of the engine, "Bootiful day, yes?"

Jimmy nervously smiled. He watched Ward pull into the tiny car park of a restaurant just off the beachfront.

"Keep going," said Jimmy. After a couple of hundred yards, Jimmy got the driver to pull over and he got out.

The beach was pebbly with sunbathers lying on towels in front of a cluster of waterside restaurants. Around thirty anchored boats bobbed up and down on the blue sea, other vessels lay drunkenly on the sand where the sea had gone out.

Jimmy sat in an elevated bar opposite the restaurant where he spotted Ward reading the menu. If she had looked directly across the small beach, she would have seen him. Various Citroën and Fiat convertible taxis which are unique to Capri, pulled up, and at 1.05pm, Jimmy spotted her, dressed in a beautifully cut white crepe suit. He watched Karen Engels ascend the stone steps onto the terrace, to be shown to the table by an eager waiter, to join her co-conspirator. She looked very different from the beaten woman from five weeks before.

Jimmy paid his bill and took the short walk across the stony beach. He made his way over to their table. Ward looked up.

"Jimmy, what a lovely surprise." She said it as if he was an old friend she was delighted to see.

Karen Engels glanced up but said nothing.

"Do join us," said Ward.

The hovering waiter brought a chair over and Jimmy sat down.

"No food for me, I'm just having a drink with the ladies." He looked at Engels. "You look like you've recovered well from when I last saw you?"

"Yes, I have, thank you." She was subdued and clearly on her guard.

"Drink Sir?" Said the waiter, as he poured some wine for Engels from the bottle Ward had already ordered.

"Small lager would be fine, please."

Jimmy folded his arms and, looking at Ward, began.

"Well Lesley, I was so bowled over with the cheque, I just had to ring and thank you, but once I heard you'd quit, it made me think long and hard. Several times, I did wonder why you asked me to investigate a death when I had no experience. Was it to fail? Even when I told you to get someone else, you still insisted I continue. Then, when I met Engels at Upton Park that day, he knew I'd worked out he was alive. The only person on that day who knew what I'd found out is you, Lesley. I'm assuming you told Karen here and she told Peter Engels?"

Ward took a sip from her drink.

"Cards on the table Jimmy. I did hire you in good faith, and you were good. I had no hidden agenda. When you told me that Engels was alive, with Karen here being the beneficiary, like you, I guessed she was in on it. So, for me, it was a light bulb moment. I saw an opportunity and gave Karen a choice: I explained to her, I could either close down the investigation and we split the money, or she'd be going to jail. I'm sorry for what happened to you Jimmy, I never expected Engels would attack you. You have to appreciate, I've spent the best part of thirty-five years watching people get payouts under very spurious circumstance. I'm not getting any younger, so this is my time. Think about it, where's the harm? Yes, Peter Engels did find out through me, but you got well paid, us two got well paid, Lloyd's are re-insured, and three miserable bastards are dead."

"I take it your generous cheque was to stop me poking around?"

"Now that I admit to!" She said brazenly?"

"Karen, there's the note I found in Shit-Tats' flat, giving instructions to a Karen, that I believe led Peter Engels to his death. It wasn't Karen Watkins, his so called second wife, he'd been talking to; it was you, wasn't it?"

Karen Engels took off her expensive sunglasses and, looking at Jimmy, she said, "I never for one moment thought Peter would do what he did to you. He told me, he thought he'd killed you. That's when I knew that he'd gone too far."

She looked uncomfortable, but nonetheless continued, "I knew Nicky Taylor was waiting for Peter to pay him off. I told him where Peter was because I thought he'd work something out with him, not kill him. The day Peter's body was found, I was devastated."

"Had you not reckoned on Shit-Tats coming to you for his money?"

"I'm not that stupid, but when he came to see me, he wouldn't settle for just what he was owed, he wanted it all. When you came into the cafe, I'd just told him he was being unreasonable, and that's when he started hitting me."

"Well, if you don't mind me saying, you seem a bad judge of character. First you not knowing your ex-husband would try to kill me, then you not knowing Shit-Tats would kill Peter, and you thinking you could reason with a madman!"

Tears ran down her cheeks.

The waiter arrived with a bottle of Peroni, partly poured into a cold glass. He looked at Engels in distress and walked away looking confused.

Jimmy continued. "The day I first visited your cafe, you knew your husband was still alive?"

"Yes that's true, Peter came to see me around last November to say he was going to fake his death and as long as I would split the money with him, he'd make me the beneficiary. I told him it was a stupid idea, but I also thought that, knowing him, he might just pull it off. It was an escape you see, to the life he owed me."

The three of them sat silent for a moment.

"There is a way forward," said Jimmy.

"Well, go on," said Ward.

"You both send me £250,00 between you. I make sure it goes to the family of the poor bastard who died in that kitchen. I will tell them it's from the relatives of Peter Engels, *'who are so very sorry for the family's loss'*. Then we can all move on."

Karen Engels wiped her eyes for a moment and said,

"I'm sure we can agree to that can't we Lesley?"

Ward thought for a moment.

"What if I say no? The payout's been made, and do you really think the authorities are going to believe an ex-con like you?"

"You wanna take that risk?"

"Look we'll pay, won't we Lesley?" said Karen Engels nervously.

Jimmy sat back in his chair and looked at the two women, then, leaning forward he said quietly, "Lesley, if you don't pay, you are going to jail, it's that simple"

"You think you're a clever bastard, don't you Jimmy?"

"Ah Lesley, you disappoint me, especially as I thought we were such old pals. I'm shocked."

The three of them sat looking at each other. Jimmy reached inside his jacket pocket and slipped a card under his beer bottle.

"My solicitors' name and bank details are on the card. If the money doesn't turn up in seven days, I get the police in."

Jimmy stood up and buttoned his jacket.

"Well, ladies it's been an absolute pleasure. And Lesley, I do hope you enjoy retirement."

"Fuck off!" Ward snarled.

He was sure Ward had no regrets.

"Enjoy your lunch," he said.

Back at his hotel, Jimmy packed and checked out, and as he looked at the sea on his journey back to Naples, he wondered if something good could happen after all.

CHAPTER TWELVE

Two Out of Three Ain't Bad

Two days later around ten in the morning, Jimmy was turning into Eastcastle Street, which is in the heart of the West End rag trade. It's about a half hour drive from Primrose Hill in heavy traffic. The yellow van behind him seemed to be tail-gating him. He lowered the sun visor. *It's going to be a nice day*, he thought.

On the car radio, the ancient DJ Jimmy Young announced in his old-school voice: "It's Elvis Costello with 'I don't want to go to Chelsea.'" As the car slowly moved forward, his body suddenly lifted. Instinctively he raised his hands as his head hit the windscreen, cutting the back of his hands. He slumped back down onto his seat. For a few seconds, he'd passed out. As he came to, he realised something had hit the back of the Cortina. A huge ham-sized fist came through the open window and hit him hard in the face, throwing him onto the passenger seat. Blood went everywhere from his exploded lip. The ham-hand then tugged impatiently at the driver's door, reaching inside trying to open it, but the impact had jammed it shut.

Jimmy scrambled out of the passenger side. Startled and dazed, he fell onto the pavement. Onlookers froze and watched as he got up and staggered along Margaret Street with the huge assailant chasing him. Just as Jimmy was starting to gain distance in Newman Street, a silver Mercedes crashed up onto the pavement in front of him. It was Palermo Frankie himself. It was unusual for him to come out to do the dirty work himself.

Jimmy swerved around him and ran across Oxford Street, then into Poland Street towards Soho. He was running literally for his life. After around a minute, he stopped and turned, his hands on his knees and breathing heavily. Jogging towards him was Fontana, who was quick for his age. Jimmy turned and ran down an L-shaped alleyway that came to a dead end behind some shops. Jimmy stood there, surrounded by high grey walls, bins and rubbish. He heard footsteps, but he had nowhere to go. Palermo was standing there, about eighty feet away, breathing heavily.

Palermo stood about thirty feet from Jimmy and said, "Well, well, well. There's no one here, just you and me son."

He dropped his hand in a quick movement and a flick knife opened.

"Just like the old days this, cutting up cocky bastards like you Jimmy."

The look of mad joy on his faced suddenly turned to anguish. He dropped down on one knee and then fell on his side. Jimmy tentatively moved towards him. He watched as Palermo's eyes blinked in slow motion. Kneeling next to him, he could hear heavy breathing, but there was no movement. Palermo's twitching hand no longer gripped the knife, he was grey in complexion. Jimmy moved closer and whispered in his ear.

"Frankie mate, I think you're having a heart attack, I saw plenty of 'em in prison. Now usually, the drill is to perform CPR and call for help. Now that may be good for your health, but I'm not so sure that it would be good for mine, so let's just see what God's decided to do with you."

Jimmy moved back and leant against a wall, lit a cigarette and waited.

"Frankie, I'm just gonna sit here like we're old mates having a chat." There was no movement from Palermo.

Jimmy continued, "Kind of madness to think of the number of guys you left dying round the back of pubs, clubs and alleyways, and here you are amongst a load of fuckin' wheelie bins about to die in the same way! All that money ain't gonna save you now is it, you old bastard?"

As Jimmy finished his sentence, a pool of urine spread under Palermo's body. Jimmy got up and stood over to the body and felt for a pulse: Palermo was dead. Jimmy stared, looking at one of the last of the 'sixties hardmen, lying there in his own piss. *Justice*, thought Jimmy.

He sat there for maybe ten minutes. Did he feel guilty? Not at all, just relief. Was it finally over? He hoped so.

He walked to the end of the alleyway leading into Beak Street, where people were rushing by, getting on with their busy lives. He entered a café and sat down. An elderly waitress wearing a check-patterned nylon dust coat and a cigarette hanging from the corner of her mouth came over to him.

"Gawd, what's happened to you love? You look like a bag of spanners!"

"Car accident," he panted.

"Cuppa?"

"Yes please," said Jimmy.

Jimmy sat there in the café trying to calm himself down. He patted his lip with a tissue. The waitress returned and put a white mug of tea in front of him.

"Sugar's on the table love, give me a shout if you want sumfink to eat."

Jimmy nodded. His lips were so sore he struggled with the hot tea.

After fifteen minutes, he saw the yellow Transit that had smashed into him drive past. In the passenger seat was Bullet Head. *So, it was his fists Jimmy had felt.* He walked back to Eastcastle Street. His car had been pushed to the side of the road and the police were in attendance. It was obviously a write-off. He kept his distance and called a cab back to the East End.

His dad opened his front door and said, "Fuck me Jimmy, what's happened?"

"Nothing to worry about Dad, just a shunt in the car, just a bit shaken up." He saw no point in recounting what had happened.

"Just going upstairs for a lie down."

Jimmy's dad watched him anxiously as he slowly went up. At 4pm, he was woken by his sister.

"Jimmy, DI Wilson's downstairs."

Jimmy sat up on the edge of the bed and rubbed his eyes. *Fuckin' hell* he thought. He slipped his shoes on and went downstairs. In the lounge sitting opposite each other, were Wilson and Mason drinking tea.

"Ah, isn't this nice Jimmy, your old man said his little boy was resting. We've got a few questions for you."

Jimmy sat down, his sister sat next to him on the setee.

"What happened to your lip," asked Wilson.

"I was in a car accident this morning."

"Wilson nodded, "Yeah, I heard. You were seen running away from it, being chased by a large male adult. I believe your car is a GREY Cortina WDE 914F, is that right?"

"Yes, a van hit me and the guy inside it looked like he was gonna murder me, so I ran!"

Mason interrupted.

"Well, nearby we found an abandoned Mercedes belonging to Palermo Frankie, whose body was found down an alleyway nearby. You know anything about that?"

"Haven't got a clue about that, Mason."

"Sort of a coincidence wouldn't you say?"

Jimmy shrugged. "Yeah, guess so."

"You're taking the piss, son, I know you was there."

"Not me."

"One of these days, I'm gonna take great pleasure in nicking you, Watson," said Wilson.

"Well, keep trying."

Wilson pulled himself up from the old worn armchair, and Mason rose from his.

"Let's go Mason."

As they left, his dad said, "What you gonna do now son?"

"Sleep!"

*

May turned to June and Jimmy hadn't had a drink for a month. He was busy doing his flat up when there was a knock at the door. He put his brush on the top of the paint tin. It was Simon, his solicitor.

"Tried to ring, but your phone's not working."

"The GPO are coming today to fix it, finally getting the place back straight. It's nice to be back to normal. Don't stand there – come in."

"No thanks, I'm on my way to court. I've finally had the chap identified that died in Engels' kitchen. He was reported missing by his wife in Barbados. You were right, he was an old friend of Engels from his school days. He'd been working as a waiter in the restaurant since it opened. The wife confirmed he'd been unwell and given no more than six months to live. He had an ex and three daughters living in Edinburgh. The good news is £150,000 was transferred to his family this morning and £100,000 to his wife in Barbados. Jimmy smiled with satisfaction.

"Got to say Jimmy, It was a nice move on your part. Oh, and by the way, a friend of yours has asked me to represent him. Do you know a Bob McGuire? There's a warrant out for his arrest but he's fled to Marbella."

"What's Handbag doing there?"

"Oh, you obviously haven't heard? The United Kingdom's extradition treaty with Spain has just run out after two hundred years. Every wanted villain in the country that hasn't been arrested is setting up shop there!"

"Bloody hell, I warned Bob, but he obviously didn't listen!"

"Looks like I'm going to be busy as there'll be plenty of plea bargains and deals being offered from the Costa del Sol. You interested in being our man in Marbella?"

Jimmy thought for a moment. He still had to pay Champagne back, sort out what he wanted to do for a living, not to mention cutting down on the booze. If he achieved two of those three, it wouldn't be so bad. And Spain would certainly be interesting.

"How long is the flight?" smiled Jimmy.

THE END

The Chapters

What Did I do Last Night- Dave Edmunds

Dreadlock Holiday- 10CC

Nutted By Reality – Nick Lowe

Airport- The Motors

Mystery Dance- Elvis Costello

Grey Cortina – Tom Robinson

Down At The Doctors- Dr Feelgood

Message in a Bottle – The Police

With A Little Luck- Wings

Burn Baby Burn (Disco Inferno) – The Trammps

Holiday In The Sun – The Sex Pisto;s

Two Out Of Three Ain't Bad – Meat Loaf

Printed in Great Britain
by Amazon